THE MINER STORIES
BOOK FIVE

Black Cloud: The MINER BOOK FIVE

S.E. McKenzie

DEDICATION
To all those left out in the cold.

This book is a book of Fiction.

TABLE OF CONTENTS

CHAPTER 1:...1

WHO DONE IT? 1

CHAPTER 2:...62

TWO RACES: THE MINESE AND THE BUYNESE 62

CHAPTER 3:...76

SIZING THINGS UP 76

CHAPTER 4...92

JACKSON AND DIANNE FIND MATHEW'S CAMERA............................92

CHAPTER 5:...96

ARE G.O.D. BOTS IN CONTROL OF WEATHER, NOW?........................96

CHAPTER 6:...126

A MAJOR DISCOVERY UNDER COLD FEET MOUNTAIN 126

CHAPTER 7:...128

WHO IS MANIPULATING THE WEATHER? 128

CHAPTER 8:...142

WHO IS STEALING THE CLOUDS?..142

CHAPTER 9:...150

CAN YOUNG BLOOD SLOW DOWN AGING?...................................150

CHAPTER 10:...153

WHO IS STONEWALLING? 153

CHAPTER 11:...159

TUNNELS, BRIDGES AND AWAKENINGS 159

CHAPTER 1:

Who Done It?

March 17th 2031, around 3:00 PM: "Why are you making my question so complicated? Mathew is either dead or alive, there is nothing in between, and John why are you reading President Peel's tweets, while I am speaking?" James Coaltonstone, one of the major principals of the Big Seven Coal Group asked. As John continued to read President Peel's tweets James banged his coffee cup on the table so hard, Mayor Stern's secretary Susan Jones was surprised that it didn't shatter.

"John, what is more important than listening to me?" James asked.

"President Peel's tweets. I heard that there is going to be a surprise military draft lottery and it is going to be shown on President Peel's live Twitter feed. I am watching to see whose numbers will be coming up," John Bell, head of security of the Big Seven Coal Group explained.

"Not much of a surprise if you already know, John. President Peel's Twitter feed will still be there, when this

1

meeting is concluded, so pay attention. These matters which are about to be discussed are important to national security and to Mathew's future, if he is still alive," Mayor Stern said.

"I have my doubts that the boy is still alive, if he is alive he could be badly injured, and possibly suffering a fate worse than death," John said.

"I know Mathew would find a way to stay alive. If he found options to survive, he would have taken them. I believe that Mathew is still alive. Even with all the crap he has been dealt, I know Mathew would persevere and stay in this world for as long as he could. Mathew always wanted to make the world a better place," Susan said.

"On another important issue, we should make it a high priority, as a security measure, to not allow any riffraff draft dodgers to hang around our park benches," John said.

"Well, if they haven't been called up yet, we should leave those kids alone, so they can enjoy our beautiful park benches while they still can. They won't be young and able forever," Mayor Stern said.

"President Peel must be having an afternoon nap I haven't seen a new tweet since this morning and I found this morning's tweet very disturbing. Amending our constitution, and then informing the public through a tweet that the core of all our constitutional rights has just been adjusted to fit reality. No discussion, nothing. And to amend our constitutional rights from having the right to 'life, liberty and the pursuit of happiness' to having the right to 'life, liberty and the pursuit of money', is very disturbing," Susan Jones said.

"Isn't having the right to the pursuit of happiness the same as having the right to the pursuit of money? What difference does it make?" James asked.

"Of course having the right to the pursuit of happiness and having the right to the pursuit of money are two entirely different things. The pursuit of money doesn't lead to a feeling of eternal happiness, for one thing," Susan said.

"Eternal happiness? What does that even mean?" John said.

"Eternal happiness is a quality of life that authoritarian people can't grasp I suppose," Susan replied.

"You, liberals kill me?" John said.

"Well, at least we don't go around killing boys like Mathew and men like Ginger Goodwin," Susan retorted.

"That is not fair, Susan." John said.

"Of course I am being fair. We are being forced to walk on eggshells all the time when we have to interact with authoritarian authorities. They ask us why anything matters because for them our quality of life doesn't matter. The meanest even laugh as people start decaying in all this rot and chaos. Happiness is relative to conditions, so it is not just happiness that matters, but the conditions and the huge gap between the rich and the poor makes me very unhappy. It all matters. This new authoritarian authority has to be in control of everything and undermines anyone below them in the social hierarchy. We all wonder why Pitville has become such a shithole place to live in," Susan began to say before James interrupted her.

"I don't wonder, the problem is the same in the entire Tut territory. All the power is centralized and benefits the few, paid for by the people. Our republic is no longer what it was, it is no longer being designed for the people by the people," James said.

"Are you sure it ever was?" Susan asked.

"No I am not sure. Especially not at a time when personhood was granted based on demographics, not automatically given because it was the humane thing to do," James said.

"I love Tut territory. This territory has been wonderful for me. I am very happy here. I have no idea why you would want to call Pitville a shithole place," John said.

"Well, stop wondering and start caring about the quality of experience you, a person with authority, are creating

3

for another person below you, like me. The entire equation lacks equity, for a start," Susan retorted.

"People, please," Mayor Stern interjected, tapping his desk with his official gavel to emphasis his own authority.

"Places turn into shit holes when the duty of governance is taken over by a bunch of grumpy old people who call themselves the Exclusion League, and who boast of conquests they will be very lucky to ever have again. I refuse to be held back by such people. I will continue to look forward to my newest adventure, which will make me the first person on the entire planet to unite Eurasia with North America through my new Hyper-loop rail, which I will be branding as a peace-connector service," James said.

"I love that idea," Susan said as she clapped. "Do you really think President Peel will allow you to make such a peace connector between Eurasia and North America?" Susan asked.

"Allow me?" James asked.

"We are technically at war with Mina?" Susan asked.

"Which is why we need my peace connector service, as a peace offering. President Peel and his Exclusion League fools people into believing they are insiders of his movement, but they are only the legs. The real insiders are a very select group, in President Peel's circle, and they look down at all outsiders, even those that vote for them," James said.

"It is so obvious when you are already an outsider, I try to tell people that, but they won't listen. For President Peel, it is all about politics and walling in the insiders from the outsiders. You can feel the culture of the wall all around us. President Peel pretends that he is talking to people on twitter, but he is really talking at them. The Twitter medium feels so intimate that many people begin to believe that they too are insiders," Susan said.

"I don't go for that kind of personality cult, myself. I have much bigger visions and aspirations. I will be the first person on the planet to finish building such a service if President Peel just leaves me alone. I am James Coaltonstone, and no one, especially President Peel, will be holding me back. We are at war with the current Mina government, not with the Minese people. Not offering a peace offering is a missed opportunity and a chance to prevent an ugly escalation to the mindless war. How is President Peel going to stop me?" James replied.

"President Peel might tweet about you, and call you a traitor or something like that," Susan said.

"President Peel might even arrest you," John said.

"All great visionaries have their share of frightening critics. I live in the land of the brave and the free, or at least I used to, and I will not be intimidated into missing an opportunity which could actually bring world peace and end world hunger," James said.

"End world hunger, isn't that a bit of stretch, James?" Mayor Stern asked.

"Absolutely not, my new rail service will able to travel up to, and maybe one day beyond 600 MPH, anywhere and everywhere. We will expand everyone's comparative advantage, which will make the world great again," James said.

"What happens if President Peel starts to come after you? Susan asked.

"I will just have to deal with that problem when the time comes. If I am arrested, I will write my memoirs from my cell, and you Susan could moonlight as my secretary, then after 'My Way' becomes a best seller, I may just run for president myself and go after Peel," James said.

"With all joking aside, James, time is not on Mathew's side. We need to find a way to find him and bring him home," Mayor Stern said.

"President Peel will definitely tweet his displeasure out to the world and his millions of followers," Susan said.

"I haven't seen any new tweets since President Peel's morning tweets, which reported that he amended our great constitution. These changes threaten the very nature of our republic," James said.

"That is exactly what I am talking about. I am finding President Peel's tweets are getting more depressing and frightening. Sometimes after I read them, I feel like the End Days are upon us. I am glad that President Peel hasn't written anything new for a few hours," Susan said.

"Twitter is down," John said.

"I am not surprised. The whole country must have logged on to read President Peel's tweet announcing his amendment to our constitution," Susan said.

"President Peel uses Twitter as he is both speaking and writing to the public. Most of the great movers tend to engage the public with powerful speeches, never just by writing, unless the writer wrote the speech, then we never really know who the writer really is," John said.

"President Jack Kennedy, from America, moved a lot of people by his writing. I own 'Profiles in Courage'. I have been reading that book a lot lately," Susan replied.

"Susan, you don't get it. Twitter combines the two mediums of writing and the real time aspects of speaking, which is why Twitter is such a huge people mover. You can actually feel President Peel in the same room as you are in. We have never had a president who shares his presence with everyday people, the way he does," John said.

"Twitter is the perfect tool for megalomaniacs," Susan said.

"John, I am your employer, not President Peel. Am I correct? In fact we hired President Peel to be our president, to represent us on the world stage and to engage in fair trade not a trade war," James said.

"Yes sir," John replied.

"Then pay attention to this meeting. Don't allow President Peel to channel your energy from this room, because he will. He is centralizing people's focus and energy, and is shamelessly growing his own monopoly of power and culture with every tweet he makes. President Peel, and his Exclusion League backers, are threatening the very principles of our republic, governance by the people for the people, to keep the people free from tyranny," James said.

"Just look at John. He can't keep his eyes off Twitter. I think, President Peel has succeeded in centralizing John's energy, Mr. Coaltonstone," Susan said.

"Peel's strategy is not going to trap me or anyone of my employees, if I can help it. People are forgetting who they are and how the power of centralized government depletes f wealth and self-worth from the people's very existence. That is why we rebelled against such tyrants who allowed themselves to be cocooned and insulated from the world and the suffering around them," James said.

"Mathew was brought up, believing in those principles. He was naturally brave, because that was his nature. When Mathew was flyking, felt free as a bird. Mathew loved freedom, and then either Jethro or Bill, shot Mathew down, out of senseless paranoia," Susan said.

"Sorting out who shot Mathew down will be much easier than finding out where he is, at this point," John said.

"Sometimes I think we would be better off with two opposing super powers. When there is only on super power, they act like the greatest nation on Earth, and boss everyone else around. The real tragedy is, we never knew what we could have been. While monopoly on power monopolizes everything and everyone, it also holds back innovation by making it too expensive to do the research. All these new tariffs and counter tariffs are going to assassinate my markets," James grumbled.

"I am starting to wonder the same thing. Having one public body, who is free from any meaningful opposition, has the power to bully and deplete the rest of us of our dignity and sense of self-worth," Susan said.

"I refuse to be diminished by anyone. I will not let President Peel and his Exclusion League backers wall me in by their prejudicial rhetoric. I am about to actualize my dream of uniting Eurasia with North America through my hyper-loop rail peace connector, which is being completed, as we speak," James said.

"Not everyone likes or even thrives under President Peel's style of governance," Susan said.

"Especially not me. While I am growing my markets, President Peel's policies are assassinating them. Negotiating with that man, is a hopeless cause," James said.

"I don't think showing mercy and consideration to other people comes naturally to megalomaniacs," Susan said.

"Without showing consideration and fairness, people feel exploited, diminished, and alienated from the institutions that govern them. I certainly do. I refuse to be socially engineered into a failure and a second class citizen of any sort," James said.

"If I were as powerful as you, Mr. Coaltonstone, I would feel the same way. President Peel's decisions grow to be more demanding and one-sided every day," Susan said.

"People who live under such regimes, lose their independence, creativity and sense of personhood. Living in a society where the few are allowed to tyrannize the majority, day after day, will only socially engineer a society of slaves," Susan said.

"President Peel isn't like that?" John said.

"Isn't he?" Susan questioned.

"I refuse to make a bad deal with anyone, I prefer no deal than a bad deal," James said.

"Could this meeting please come to order? John, please start showing some respect to the people who are actually physically in this room with you and are very aware of your existence," Mayor Stern interjected again, as he tapped his desk with the mayor's official gavel several times.

"I thought I was in order, Sir," John said.

"Let's get on with it," James interjected.

"I expect that from now on, this meeting will stay in order. I agree with James that Mathew is either dead or alive, and we need to find him as soon as we can. It is not up to us to decide for Mathew if he is better off dead. Even if his injuries are life transforming, we still have an obligation to find Mathew, and give him every opportunity available to make his own life choices while overcoming any new challenge he may have to face," Mayor Stern said.

"Many people would disagree that there is nowhere in between life and death. My guess is that those are the same people who never see the missed opportunities which could prevent wars. Of course there are terrible fates worse than death, but I agree, it is up to Mathew to decide for himself, what conditions would make his life no longer worth living. He loved this world, and he would not leave it, prematurely, without a fight. Especially now, with fears of a new race war being propagated by President Peel through his Twitter feed, a lot of people are wondering if death is really the worst option they have," Susan said.

"Those people are cowards and sick," John said.

"I know Mathew would always choose life over death, and he would never leave this world voluntarily," James said.

"I agree, Mathew loved this world and he would fight with all his might to stay here. Those people, our people, who are terrified, feel conflicted and fear for their futures, are growing in numbers. For some people, personal integrity is everything, and they would rather die, than betray themselves. You were the one, John, who brought up the subject of 'some life conditions are worse than death'. For some people constant fear is one of those life conditions," Susan said.

"Yes, but I was putting those conditions in a different context than this sick twist you just added to my words," John replied.

"People please, this is supposed to be a planning meeting to help Mathew return to the life he had here in Tut territory, before this unfortunate accident happened. Let us please stay on task. I would like to add that I know when times get hard, I have no idea where I would be, without Martha,

Mrs. Stern. Does Mathew have a love interest, a girl friend?"
Mayor Stern asked.

"He certainly does not," James said.

"I think he does," Susan said. "Maria once mentioned a little girl, Mathew has known since they were toddlers. She mentioned that they were getting closer as they grew older.'

"John are you still reading President Peel's tweets?" I told you to pay attention to this meeting," James ordered.

"Every time I see John reading those tweets, I am reminded of that horrible feeling I get. It feels like I am under a gun, or under some curse or some dark power is lingering over my head and then lands right inside my head. President Peel is not my president, he doesn't represent my values. I wish there were cooler heads watching over our territory. Those two hot heads are still floating around on that nuclear sub, spying on everything and everyone. Jethro and Bill don't represent my values either," Susan said.

"You are sick, Susan," John said with obvious disdain.

"This is what I am talking about," Mayor Stern said. "We must stay on task. Time is of the essence in every search and rescue mission. This one is no different or less important. We must focus on our common goal, which is to bring Mathew home."

"I agree. We really have to focus on a positive team outcome, because that is in Mathew's best interest. It is very hard when those tweets take over the room, they feel so negative and seem to guzzle up all your energy and time. I get incredibly anxious and then I feel empty of any future ambition after I read President Peel's tweets. I get a similar feeling after being glared at by one of his cronies from the Exclusion League. I feel this super negative energy lingering in my head, and then I can't seem to get it out of my head. That is when I find playing my etherplayer music so helpful. So far, I only get those super negative feelings for around half an hour, at the most. There are many other people that say they feel the same way after reading those tweets or getting glared at by those Exclusion League cronies, for hours. Some feel bad for days," Susan said.

"Well they are all sick," John said.

"Usually there is a cause for sickness. People are now preparing for the End Times instead of preparing for their future and their family's future. We must remember that Mathew deserved a future. He was deserving of a great future," Susan said.

"Putting the Tut territory first is a great idea. I heard that President Peel is going to demand that all Minese, residing in Tut territory, wear the letter 'M' on their left breast, the place closest to their heart. This policy is for the good of national security, so we can tell the Minese apart from everyone else. Once we know who they are, we can choose to either target them or to ignore them. Anyone wearing an 'M' will be served last, allowing the rest of us to be served first," John said.

"And what could possibly go wrong? Our currency gets boycotted or devalued through hyperinflation? Promising jobs for youth to assist in enslaving and starving our perceived inferiors can't result in anything good, Sir. Any cruel action could result in an even crueler reaction, and possibly even a cruel, lingering and slow death," Susan Jones said.

"President Peel is supposed to be tweeting his new innovative government policies today, but it is already way past three in the afternoon," John said.

"Could Mina force us to pay the trillions of dollars in debt that we owe them, in retaliation?" Susan asked.

"I really don't know, Susan?" Mayor Stern said.

"Could Mina actually foreclose on the Tut territory?" Susan asked.

"That would be like declaring war on us," James said.

"But Mina has already declared war on us," Susan said.

"Mina declared war on us because we declared war on them. And after this war, who knows who we will all be. We might need to change our identities, if our government is blamed for millions of deaths and mass starvation, I too would say that President Peel is not my president," James said.

"It is impossible to foreclose on a country. All we would have to do is print a bunch of money and buy up all of the Treasury Bills that Mina owns, and doesn't want to roll over," John said.

"Or we could prevent this war from escalating by overthrowing President Peel and the Exclusion League backers while staying true to ourselves. Is this war even necessary? Why do competing cultures have to clash against each other so hard?" James asked.

"Mr. Coaltonstone what you just suggested sounds like treason?" John asked.

"Really? Asking 'what is it we are fighting for?' and asking 'if this war is necessary?' treason? John one day we will be asked these same questions. Was this war really necessary and why didn't we just overthrow President Peel and prevent the latest Great War? Should we answer the questions now or after a million people are killed and millions more have lost limbs? Since when was any war really great?" James asked.

"I agree with James. So why not question the whole process?" Susan asked.

"No one wants to be called a traitor, especially not on Twitter. I am reading his tweets all the time, I know the impact those tweets have on people and their families. And I know there are some people who should not be in charge of their own lives, and the Brotherhood should be taking charge. At times, personal autonomy is not in the national interest," John said.

"Exactly, you are being controlled by President Peel's tweets because of your fear of being called a traitor. Do we really want to be controlled by our fear instead of being influenced by the content of our character and our visions to make our personal futures great? Why are we even wasting money, my money, the people's money on war when we could all be working together on a current project which is dearest to my heart, my Bering Strait Hyper-Loop rail Peace Complex," James said.

"Who has ever heard of building peace connectors during war time?" John asked.

"It is the people building peace connectors that prevent wars. Finding ways to work as a global team to better everyone's lives, always leads to interesting and well-paying jobs. What kind of incentive is President Peel offering to inspire greatness? Can he offer anything positive or constructive, at all?" Susan said.

"My hyper-loop rail service is going to change the world. It will break time related travel barriers. Thousands of people will travel from North America to Eurasia and back at over 600 PMH," James said.

"All President Peel does is tweet negative comments to people, wasting everyone's time and making them upset and angry. And I always wonder if I will be me, next. Now, he is going to impose the lottery draft on our young people, who will be glued to twitter, waiting for their numbers to come up. President Peel's plan is to draft our youngsters and forcing them to kill and maim other youngsters, in faraway worlds and to act like death squads here at home, repulses me. John are you on my side or on President Peel's side?" James asked.

"I voted for you sir, I am on your side. I know you provide me with a good job. You were good to my late brother and our family after my brother passed away. You also provide Jethro and Bill with good jobs. They should be on your side too, Sir," John said.

"Exactly. I am your job creator. And time is money. President Peel is not just wasting everyone's time with his negativity, he is also wasting everyone's potential to make money. My hyper-loop rail network will break time barriers not make time barriers that everyone glued to Peel's Twitter feed is doing. I have seen people stop everything, ignoring people that they are with, to read those tweets. John what are you doing?"

"I am reading President Peel's tweets," John said.

"Not in my meeting you are not," Mayor Stern protested.

"My new hyper-loop rail service will be changing the world and I will be leaving that idiot Peel behind in coal dust. My new rail service will save everyone tons of money and time when traveling and shipping products between North America and Eurasia. My new rail service will shock and awe on a global scale, and in a positive way," James said.

"James your visions have always been ahead of our time. I am feeling claustrophobic just thinking of traveling so fast in a capsule. I do enjoy train travel, but at a slower pace, where I can order a meal and look out of the window and watch the scenery go by. Traveling at speeds up to 600 MPH in a capsule type tube, I find rather terrifying," Mayor Stern said.

"It is no different than riding the roller coaster at Pitville Fall Fair Sir, but faster, has less hills and the ride lasts a lot longer. When you exit the ride, you and your freight are in another continent. I find the idea very exciting, almost exciting as this new war we are involved in at present," John said.

"We also have viewing screens inside and cameras outside, so we can see the scenery, though it will be going by rather fast," James said.

"I think we should be focusing on new projects instead of getting all caught up in this war mongering and rivalry," Susan said.

"Exactly, Susan. My project is not ahead of our time. President Peel is behind the times. We are building my hyper-loop rail network as we speak. We, my organization, will be moving forward into the future. Peel is pulling us backwards, which is very annoying. John, will you stop reading those tweets, and listen to me," James said.

"I know what you are saying, James," Mayor Stern said. "It is hard, or maybe even impossible to determine whether someone is insane when all they are doing is using Twitter to feud with people, some very high profile people. On the other hand, it is very easy to tell when someone is being creative or destructive. At first, President Peel's tweets were entertaining like a reality show, but feuding with volatile world leaders, to increase Twitter ratings, in real life, I find terrifying. It is easy enough to determine if a person's actions are evil and destructive, because any outcome of such action will be measurable. And if a person doesn't care who he harms, he shouldn't have access to weapons of mass destruction or any sort of supreme power,"

"I am a patriot. My country comes first. What is good for my side will not be good for the other side. If we blow up the other side, we will be better off," John said.

"Will we really?" Wouldn't we be better off, on both sides, if we just banned the bomb and agree to build peace connectors and trade fairly with each other? The real competitor these days, is not so much humans against humans for jobs, it is human against bots," James said.

"Or if we can't do that, we could just leave each other alone to live lives, peacefully, in parallel worlds," Susan said.

"Susan, don't be so naïve. We ban the bomb, the other side doesn't, they win and we lose. That is human nature. Treaties are cancelled all the time. These days, treaties can even be cancelled live on Twitter," John said.

"Will we always be doomed to live in such an insane society? No wonder Mathew felt so great when he was flyking above all this tension and madness. I agree with James, we should be thankful that we have the know-how to be building peace connectors. And I am glad James is building them while our President, I should say the President, I don't feel like he is representing my interests at all, is escalating tensions between opposing cultures. The only thing transparent about President Peel, is that he is taking advantage of the fact that we are already socially engineered to clash against each other," Susan said.

"I grew up in a school where we had very rich kids and very poor kids. You know what the rich kids did, to torment the poor kids? The poor kids didn't even have enough money to buy lunch in the school cafeteria, so instead of the rich kids giving the poor kids their extra change, they actually glued dollar bills to the floor and watched the poor kids tear at them to bits. I used to watch the rich kids hide behind the corner, filming those poor kids, tearing apart the dollar bills glued to the floor. The rich kids used their fancy com-phones to video those kids tearing up the dollar bills glued to the floor. The rich kids would be zooming in on the poor kids' faces, then they would put those videos on social media. That is human nature," John said.

"And didn't that behavior show you that compassion elevates humanity from madness?" Mayor Stern asked.

"Hell no, that behavior taught me why it is so important to never be so dirt poor," John said. "Especially when the hall monitors, other rich kids of course, gave those poor kids detentions and sometimes even got them suspended from school."

"I swore to myself that I would never let anyone squash me like a bug just for a joke, the way those poor kids were squashed just to entertain the rich kids. I have always known that money is the true equalizer, and at least the bots don't discriminate, unless they are programmed to," John said.

"Spoken like a true patriot," James said.

"Strange how much President Peel is behaving like those rich kids," Susan said.

"We all know President Peel could be insane. You know President Peel's policies defy reality, at times. Just read his tweets," James said.

"I am, but I don't see any new ones," John said.

"John, I didn't mean read them now. Take a minute and reflect upon our situation. Consider the world we are about to lose," James said.

"I believe this New Social Order will be better for me, it will create more jobs, and show people who is boss," John said.

"That is the way the centralized system works, and it will not be doing its dirty work on me. The centralized system excludes people, by design, but it has never been able to exclude me. It is all about social engineering. From the moment you are able to walk and talk, they are defining who you are and who you can be. Through their relentless programming and by giving you very little free time, your curiosity about everything is so dull, bots are comparatively much better at responding and connecting appropriately than militaristically institutional people are. And that is how we are being enslaved, and Mathew refused to be enslaved that way. At times, he was as free as a bird and refused to grow desponded the way many young people do his age. Mathew was a winner in his own way," James said.

"He sure learned to be close to nature. He was so kind to the wild animals and often I saw him share his lunch with them," Susan said.

"We, the people must account for all the missed opportunities we will have, if we do not try to prevent this mindless war. We should be always aware of what we are losing," James said.

"We have to remember how this New Social Order is effecting the young people," Susan said.

"The future generations will one day ask us, if President Peel really knew what he was doing, and if he didn't know what he was doing, why didn't we stop him? President Peel's tariffs and Mina's counter-tariffs are causing hyperinflation and terrible hardship for the poorest families in Tut territory. Whose side is Peel on? Does he want to create a crash, an economic depression? President Peel's refusal to see out of the box is infuriating. I know tariffs in a roundabout way are replacing the corporate income taxes we were always complaining about, but these tariffs have not just led to counter-tariffs, but now we have this hostility, possibly irreversible, between nations. Tariffs do not grow wealth between nations because expanding the economy becomes impossible. To radically decrease the capacity of our own economy while using federal government financing models that worked over two hundred years ago, during a time when the internet and jet travel were nonexistent, is insanity. I can't wonder what side President Peel is really on. Does he really want to bankrupt the Tut territory, and make it impossible for us to finance the war? At worse the tariffs and counter-tariffs will box us in economically, while other countries grow their comparative advantage while expanding their markets," James argued.

"And how are we expected to win this war, once our currency loses its value, as we waste resources fighting a trade war? Why is the president taking us back to fiscal policies that may have worked over two hundred years ago, but could ruin us in this modern age?" Mayor Stern asked.

"But wasn't this country founded on tariffs? Didn't the federal government finance its operations through tariffs for almost a hundred years, before it brought in income tax to finance its operations?" John asked.

"So what? Why are we comparing apples with oranges? The times have changed drastically since then. And whoever is trying to convince us that we would be better of returning to those times, without internet, without speedy global travel and communications, is deceiving us," Mayor Stern said.

"This country was founded on the principle that it was not right or fair to tax people who had no representation. Taxation without representation is being forced onto the illegals and vagrants, of today. They pay all kinds of sales tax but are always treated like dogs," James said.

"The government imposes self-serving duties all the time, Sir, in one way or another, to fight its wars," Susan interjected.

"Yes, but most modern governments take into consideration their comparative advantage so they can expand their markets while moving forward into the next century. Only a fool would want to contract the national economy and go backwards two centuries, forcing the population into idleness and poverty, which used to be unknown to the modern world," James said.

"The government also knows how well the Pea Act went. It contributed to the justification of violent revolution and civil war, in many people's minds," John said.

"I still hate peas," Mayor Stern added.

"I do too," Susan said.

"I have always believed that it was my patriotic duty to hate peas," John said.

"As we know, adding duty tax to give an overseas company an advantage, was the last straw; the proverbial straw that broke the camel's back. Only fools would repeat such dismal history. The federal government used tariffs to fund itself and to pay off the interest on its war related debt during a time before modern governments charged income tax. Using such a draconian model will clearly lead to losing a huge comparative advantage. The importers who smuggle goods into the country, free from tariffs, are selling goods much than we can even buy them for," James noted.

"Yes, and they are committing economical treason. Their business model is unpatriotic and illegal," John said.

"Sadly I have to agree with John. A lot of those places are not paying any tax at all. These importers are now part of the black market. Why would they voluntarily pay tax on top of the tariffs and the counter-tariffs that they are already paying on goods they need to be buying for themselves?" James asked.

"What are people supposed to do? Nobody's wages are increasing to keep up with the rate of this horrible hyperinflation," Susan said.

"Who cares about the nobodies?" John asked.

"John, really," Mayor Stern scolded.

"That is exactly what I am talking about. President Peel is not acting rationally, let alone presidential. Using fiscal policy that is a couple of hundred years out of date is madness, if not fiscal suicide. This president doesn't just box his opponents into a corner, he boxes himself and us into a corner, too. Sometimes the saddest victims of demagoguery are the demagogues themselves. I would have done a much better job, if I had won the election. I certainly would not be devaluing our currency until investors decide to move their wealth into a more stable currency," James said.

"But you didn't win the election, President Peel won. Talking like this could get us all shot. Such talk sounds like treason. Whatever President Peel decides to do, is technically beyond our jurisdiction. We should continue the planning of our strategy for searching and rescuing Mathew. Shouldn't we just let the metropolis authorities worry about these complicated macro items, and we just stay focused on finding out what happened to Mathew?" Mayor Stern asked.

"Absolutely. Being able to live and invest independently from arrogant fools making tons of bad decisions is usually a big plus. As if this situation with Mathew weren't bad enough, I was sent a memo today, that the Minese Authority will be imposing a tariff on my coal and steel. The reason is said to be because the Exclusion League backers have placed tariffs on Minese coal and steel, supposedly to give my Big Seven Coal Group's steel a break. The theory probably is based on the premise that if my confidence in my market domination is increased or at least artificially sustained, I will be able to convince my shareholders that it is wise to make new capital investments during this time of war and uncertainty. My markets were naturally sustainable. I didn't need, or ask for, a President Peel's command post to artificially protect my markets in the supply chain, because my prices had a competitive advantage and created demand, all on their own. Now with tariff and counter-tariffs inflating production costs and selling costs, that President Peel is assassinating my markets and sending me back to zero. Go figure the logic out, I certainly cannot. Why would President Peel want to assassinating my markets by instigating a trade war which always leads to prices being unaffordable and cause a slowdown of the economy. How can anyone joke that a trade war is sustainable. I am immersing myself in the project of the century, and President Peel refuses to allow us to elevate to the next level of humanity and to move forward into the future," James said.

"You always move forward despite the rules, Sir," John said.

"But not usually from point zero, John. Just because we no longer have to file quarterly reports, doesn't mean that we are doing great again in Tut territory, it just means that we don't know what we don't know. We really need substance to be great, not just the look. Sure, my quarterly reports are no longer available to the financially illiterate and to the G.O.D. bots, but my shareholders are reading those reports all the time, and they are sick with worry. And when they are sick with worry, they are more prone to cut corners, and replace miners with illegals and botguards," James said.

"But you always find a way sir, to keep everything moving faster than everyone else. And isn't that the way you have to being ahead of everyone else," John said.

"My new project will move me so far ahead, everyone else will be left behind in disbelief. President Peel is bankrupt as a leader, or he wouldn't have to yell and scream and fire so many people, all the time. The Exclusion League backers said the tariffs wouldn't matter because my coal is mined on Tut Island, but I know they are lying to me. The logic doesn't fit any business model that I have been using. Since when was Tut territory the center of the universe, anyway, President Peel must be lying or fudging the numbers. It makes more sense to assume that the backers want the non-backers to go bankrupt. This trade war is the stupidest government policy I have ever heard of. Only thing stupider is this actual military war we are engaging in with the Minese government and broadcasting the military lottery draft over the president's live Twitter feed. Talk about deranged. Friendly fire from Tut Island shoots down my stepson and the Minese Authority is placing a 50% tariff on my coal, and steel because Tut Metropolis has placed a 50% tariff on Minese coal and steel. Why can't we all just get a long and make the world a better place?" James asked.

"I agree totally, Mr. Coaltonstone. It is more fun to be nice to each other. But people who dish out snide comments on Twitter, they are usually trying to show their dominance or they are showing poor judgment. All this yelling and screaming frazzles my nerves and makes me sick to my stomach. Instead of worrying about the End Times and what President Trump will be doing next, we should be exercising our constitutional right to pursuit of happiness and stay free to plan our future," Susan said.

"Which brings us back to the task at hand. Mathew had every right to feel free flyking in the sky, not worrying about getting shot down. Mathew had every right to pursue happiness while he was still young and able and not confined to crazy life insurance stipulations," James said.

"Does the constitution even apply during wartime?" John asked.

"What is wartime? War seems to be going on all the time. It starts with a bunch of grumpy old men fighting for global dominance and willing to send out young draftees to kill other young draftees, to do it, then one side surrenders, and that specific battle might stop. Maybe, President Peel should be cautious not to anger the spiritual energy surrounding us, because in the end, that is what really dominates everything. Energy doesn't die but President Peel is doing his best to convert our energy to his way of thinking. President Peel and his morning un-pleasantries may appeal to others who also want to dominate the planet with fear and unpleasantness, and while doing so, they threaten the very principles on which our republic was founded. Wartime is the most fearful and unpleasant time there is. But wartime seems to be happening all the time. It is a fact that the energy in the Tut territory is mixed with a lot of Minese, many of them died from the deeds of brutal hands. If there is some truth that angry spirits, living in the ether and clouds, can cause hail, rain and drought, I suspect that we are due for a lot of bad weather. We take life energy for granted, even though it binds us temporarily to this place on Earth and surrounds us, every day of our lives, and never dies," Susan said.

"Susan!" Shouted James Coaltonstone, Mayor Stern and John Bell at the same time.

"I am right. Energy is transformed based on source, either of love or hate. And what kind of world would we rather be living in?" Susan asked.

"Susan is right, there isn't only one way to see things or to respond. One of my pet projects has been Mutually Assured Progress, which also compliments my new rail service, which is almost complete. Mutually Assured Destruction is madness, and the philosophy seems to be relying on the archaic mentality, that 'if mine is bigger than yours, I get to win'," James said. "And only fools believe that might is best."

"We need to consider all the options and concerns, not just from the supply side, but from the demand side as well. We need to broaden our horizons and not allow us to be fooled by a simplistic 'command from high or else', mentality, that is out of balance and out of touch with everyday people," Susan said.

"I agree with Susan. There are usually several options and with today's modeling tools, it would be a tragedy to rely on simple-minded prejudice and assumptions, when making important decisions. It is no longer necessary to get trapped in a big win for one side and a big loss for the other side. The sum-zero game mentality, where the rich get richer and the poor grow so poor, they can no longer sustain themselves. Making products unaffordable will lead to my markets getting assassinated," James said.

"I do agree that we must dig deeper into the mechanics of our options so that we can gain a greater understanding of which direction our decisions may lead us to. Just considering the supply side, is the typical approach of an oligarch, and the oligarchs did not elect me to be mayor of Pitville, the people elected me," Mayor Stern said.

"Good for you Mr. Stern and Mr. Coaltonstone. There are many options, beyond just the archaic rule from high approach of a command style administration. Good leadership implies a win-win outcome, so the majority of the people are not tyrannized by the few who would love to steer us back to a command from high militaristic approach," Susan said.

"There is always the nature and nurture argument. President Peel is assuming that making it unpleasant for people beneath him, in the privilege of the New Social Order, which gives him the chance to relive his glory day of being a tough and a no nonsense boss. But he is not supposed to be just a boss, he is supposed to be our president, in a constitutional republic, which was designed for the people and by the people. A constitutional republic was supposed to be free of tyranny and domination by a certain class of people who were inheritors of fabulous amounts of wealth and property. There was supposed to be something left over for the majority of the citizens of the republic, who do most of the work," Mayor Stern said.

"What we really need is a fearless and freedom loving leader, like yourself, Mr. Stern, who inspires people to do great things, and doesn't just rely on social engineering and to justify being unpleasant to others. What I am saying is the truth. All of our energy is just borrowed, and one day it will have to be returned, either more pure or more toxic," Susan said.

"Even if you are right, Susan, much of this is way beyond our control, after all I am just a small town mayor," Mayor Stern began to say.

"Actually being nurturing to other people is solely in our control," Susan said.

"Okay, all of this speculation is beyond the scope of our meeting. We are supposed to be having a serious meeting about our national security and planning while developing the most practical and effective strategy to find out what happened to Mathew," Mayor Stern said.

"Actually, with today's modeling tools, we are much closer to being able to predict outcome than ever before. Anyway it doesn't take a rocket scientist to realize that pricing goods from a command station, backed by the military, doesn't only lead to hyper-inflation, shortages of goods, and unhappy people, it also threatens the very nature of our constitutional republic," James said.

"You see, Mr. Stern, it is not just me that is wondering if the current president is putting our republic at risk of becoming a totalitarian regime. We should be careful when we interact with people that are escalating conflicts, especially those who shoot first and think later. Rumor has it that some of the spirits surrounding us are so angry they can't let go of their attachment of this world. Many believe there are places in Pitville where the minds and the souls of the dead linger, possibly in the ether, Sir, and possibly for eternity. And when you walk near those places you can feel a chill, even on a hot muggy day," Susan said.

"Will you just shut up Susan, and stop sounding so spooky," John demanded.

"People, we must calm down," Mayor Stern said. "We know some of this secrecy behind Mathew being shot down, is necessary for national security and some of it may not be necessary. Just like being able to identify illegals is good for national security but is it really necessary that all the Minese in the Tut territory wear an 'M' on their left breast? Having to coerce people to do something against their will, would make me a ruthless tyrant, and that is not my leadership style, by any stretch. Maybe the President Peel and his Exclusion League backers won the election by promoting exclusion, but are the feds going to turn to small town municipalities for enforcement? How do they expect small town mayors to win elections or balance budgets if they refuse to act decently toward their residents? The more threatening we are to any of these targeted groups, the more threatening they could be to us," Mayor Stern asked.

"That is the nature of war, Sir," John interjected.

"I don't believe that any of this nastiness is necessary, not even for a moment. Mathew had every right to feel like he belonged. Mathew had every right to feel safe and secure, just like we all do. We all want to live in a world where we like we belong. There is a lot more to being human, than just the obvious skin deep characteristics that the self-serving Exclusion League define us by. We have our content of character which defines who we choose to be, which makes us who we are," Susan said.

"Speak for yourself, Susan. Actually, don't speak at all," John said.

"John, will I have to ask James to send you back to sensitivity training class? We can't stay strong, as a team, if we continue to tear each other apart as individuals," Mayor Stern said.

"It is not like Mathew expected the world to give him happiness, he was willing to pursue happiness for himself," James said.

"Mathew had lost so much and flyking in the sky was one place he felt that he belonged. Mathew never questioned why so many bad things happened to him, during his short life," Susan said.

"There shouldn't be a conflict between Mathew's security and our country's security. Mathew belonged in this country and had every right to be where he wanted to be, in his pursuit of happiness," Mayor Stern said.

"Maria, told me that Mathew felt free as a bird when he was flyking, and I believe that he was serving his higher purpose by just being himself," Susan said.

"No one has a higher purpose, Susan. They do what they do, and that is it. What you see, is what there is. People are just skin deep, a little bit more developed than a dog but less friendly. We suffer because that is the kind of doggy-eat-dog world we are living in. We can't find Mathew, partly because we are missing relevant information about what actually happened to him. We also have to worry about the Minese and their ghost guns and ghost ships. The Minese people have the technology to print out one gun on demand, or a thousand guns, and they can use these undocumented guns to shoot us. Next thing you know they will be able to print out 3D nuclear bombs, on demand. We are also very short on manpower since we are having to guard Coalton Two's First Bank against looters after the Cold Feet Mountain slide buried part of it," John said.

"If secrecy laws are stopping us from knowing the reasons for events that affect our lives and the lives of our loved ones, we will not be able to fight back in time to be effective. How does that make our nation more secure?" James said.

"How can we respond intelligently or even believe that we are secure, for that matter, if we don't know what is really going on around us?" Susan asked.

"I agree with Susan. This fake security has been going on for the last twenty something years. And I have never felt more insecure. The very time the public needs to be alerted about lurking danger is the very time the public is kept in the dark," James complained.

"When information about public safety is classified as 'MOST SECRET', no one knows that there is danger nearby. We continue with our lives, assuming that we are safe," Susan said.

"Don't worry Susan, you and your kind are always being watched. If you were in any danger, we would be the first to know about it. You will never know how much we know about people like you. We watch you all the time, for your own good. We and the Brotherhood are watching out for you, so don't worry your little head, Susan," John said.

"You mean you are spying on people like me? Writing reports about people like me?" Susan said.

"People, we are here to find out what happened to Mathew. Please keep your differences to yourselves. And John, you used to smile a lot more when you were participating at our meetings. You look so much like your late brother, when you smile. The way you just scowled at Susan is scaring me. Susan is opinionated, I can grant you that, but she is a loyal and competent, and always has been," Mayor Stern said.

"Thank you, Sir. It is really important to me, that Mathew is found. I don't want to hear any excuses to why national security is more important than finding Mathew," Susan said.

"I loved Mathew like a son, and I demand to know what happened to him. Any information relating to my stepson's shooting, if it must be kept classified as secret, should at least be available to the members of our search and rescue team. We need to know what happened to him so that we can find him," James said.

"Sir, I don't have anything positive to report. We are at war, Sir. We can't be transparent or our enemies will know all our secrets and will find it easier to tyrannize us. Jethro refuses to speak to us and whatever Bill tells us is out of his fear for Jethro. Jethro and Bill are contradicting each other whenever they describe what happened before and after Mathew was shot. They also are contradicting themselves, which makes it appear that they are not always telling the truth. Their stories are continually changing. Both Jethro and Bill are making our investigation as difficult for us as they possibly can, Sir," John said.

"Classic defense: 'it wasn't me, it was he'. It is terrifying that Jethro and Bill are officially on our side," Susan said.

"Susan!" John scolded.

"I hate to say it but I tend to agree with Susan. Jethro and Bill are making it very difficult for our rescue mission because they are not co-operating with our search efforts. They are behaving as if they are on the opposite side from us.

What happened to the common good, some kind of common ground, and some kind of shared values?" James asked.

"James, I know this is not official business but how are your sons, Alex and Bobby? Do you hear from them at all?" Mayor Stern asked.

"Not really, Alex took a leaf of absence and never answers his phone or the emails I send him. Whenever I try to see Bobby, I am told that he is not available," James said.

"Twenty-six years of hard labor is a long time," Susan said.

"That kind of hard time could kill Bobby," James said.

"Bobby will find a way to survive, he always does," John said.

"Bobby was my second son, and always resented not being the first. Alex on the other hand was my first son, and always resented Bobby from the day we brought him home. I will always remember Alex asking if we could take Bobby back," James said.

"You must be very proud of Bobby for taking the fall," Susan said.

"Susan, really," Mayor Stern said.

"I am actually devastated that Judge Bell ruled against Bobby so harshly. They blamed the Mine Five disaster on Bobby's engineering methods. The judge had his mind made up from the very beginning. As far as I can see the cards were stacked against Bobby before the trial even started.

"Judge Bell had little choice," John said.

"Just imagine the cards being stacked up against the entire privileged Big Seven Coal Group's administration, the way they are stacked up against us. Is that what you meant, John?" Susan asked.

"Susan you keep talking like that to us and you will be hearing from the Brotherhood. Sir, Bobby was the lead Ventilation Engineer, Judge Bell had to follow the law," John Bell said.

"Just like Judge Bell finding you not guilty of murdering Ginger Goodwin because he ruled that you shot Ginger in self-defense?" Susan asked.

"Susan, I am warning you," John said as he raised his voice.

"Please people, we are all on the same side here," Mayor Stern said.

"Are we?" Susan asked.

"Of course we are," James replied.

"Time is running out, Sir. We must continue the discussion related to the mission. It just might be this mission will turn out to be a retrieval mission. On another point, the Brotherhood are supporting Jethro and Bill's demands that their interests come first," John said.

"John, we have to search before we can rescue or retrieve. I agree, our mission would be a lot easier if Jethro and Bill would start co-operating with us and start considering the common good," Mayor Stern said.

"Mathew's best interest should come first. He is the victim here," Susan said.

"Both Jethro and Bill are very good shots and they are highly respected by the Brotherhood, Sir. Our philosophy is 'don't let the enemy shoot first'. All Tut spies have excellent training, excellent reflexes and excellent connections, Sir," John added.

"It is terrifying that those two men are on our side," Susan said.

"Susan, our national security during times of war is also about maintaining our dignity, so why don't you just shut up and let me speak first. Would you rather our world be run by the Brotherhood or by strangers?" John asked.

"You are the one to talk, Mr. Head of Security. Who was there when your twin brother, Don, was shot? Who came first then? Most likely the perp thought Don was you, which is hard to believe since he was always the better looking twin," Susan said.

"Don and John were identical. It was their expression which set them apart," Mayor Stern said.

"That is for sure. You never heard Don demand to be the first for anything," Susan said.

"Maybe if he had, he would have stayed alive for longer," John said.

"They were like that as boys too, Susan. John always demanded to be first, and Don would always let him be first, just to avoid a fight," James said.

"Don is gone, Ginger is gone, Mathew is gone, Christina is near gone," Susan began to say.

"Susan, Christina is just sleeping, and Mathew might be still alive. And don't forget baby James, he is growing bigger, every day," James said.

"We really need to stop getting so emotional," John said.

"Do you choose that condescending tone just to enrage people, who are beneath you in this New Social Order? Sometimes I wonder if you talk down to people to purposely enrage them into responding, so that you can report them to the G.O.D bots which, will marginalize them for life. Isn't that what you spies do, these days? Do you and your Brotherhood friends have a goal to meet for the donut fund?" Susan retorted back.

"Susan stop talking. I would much rather see our Brotherhood supplied with plenty of donuts and coffee than the system being run by strangers and outsiders," John replied angrily.

"People please, we must implement our strategy as a unified force. We must all stay connected and remain on the same path without clashing into each other, for the sake of the child," Mayor said.

"I agree with Ted. I have enough to worry about at the moment, so please people, please settle down and just get along," James said.

"We are on the brink of World War Three, and we are bound to feel tension, James," Mayor Stern said.

"This war was provoked and was completely preventable. That President Peel picks battles assuming he is going to win. I see little consideration or concern for those youngsters who are being drafted in an impersonal lottery, soon to be announced on Twitter, to fight his battles for him. I have to figure out what to tell Christina when she wakes up from her coma. Doctor Knight thinks she might be waking up soon, something to do with her vital signs increasing in strength. I also have to figure out how to handle Mathew's grandmother who is a very difficult woman," James Coaltonstone said sounding defeated.

"Maria is a good friend of mind," Susan interjected.

"What else needs to be said?" John asked rhetorically.

"I agree with James, we have to put our differences aside and get along. We have to focus on our objective, which is to find Mathew," Mayor Stern said.

"It is amazing we trade at all with so many people that we hate so deeply and are at war with," Mayor Stern said.

"That is the fog of war for you. Obviously the fog of war deranges the entire atmosphere by design, its purpose is to cause disorder for the New World Order while derailing the things we have grown to depend on. If we stopped trading with half the world, it would only be a matter of time that the global economies would come crashing down along with our domestic economy. That fog of reality is everywhere. That is why we must trust the Invisible Hand to hold it all in place while enemy forces all around us try to displace everything we know to be true and love. We trade as if the economy is in a different realm than the war because both sides have a necessity and a comparative advantage to continue their ties as trading partners. President Peel and the Exclusion League backers are deranging the entire process of social and economic order, on purpose. It is amazing we still have the energy wake up at all, just to face another crazy, stressful day without going bananas. If it weren't for my hyper-loop rail project I would lose myself in this void of numbness, the current political climate is causing me to feel. I have no trust in this New World Order that is dominating the Tut territory. We leave our warm beds every morning to face the cold and crazy world, without any promise of the world getting any better or kinder, any day soon. When I die, I want to be more than just a picture on a wall," James said.

"James, if it weren't for your coal, your vision, and your new hyper-loop rail service, the world would be a much colder and slower place. Your vision and energy sourcing, empower the engines of this world and without you and your ingenuity, those engines would be running out of steam, by now. Without you James, we would be like our local Minese, rummaging through things that are thrown out onto the streets on National Moving and Eviction Day, with no hope for a better life, for a better way," Mayor Stern said.

"Sir, I am sorry to change the subject, but are you certain Christina could wake up soon?" Susan asked.

"Susan, please," John Bell interjected.

"Don't Susan me, John. Mathew was a boy, who flyked in a sky that he thought he had a right to flyke in. He also might have felt safe flyking in the sky, closer to his higher power. Considering how toxic it is getting to be on the ground, you can't blame him. The possibility that Mathew's mother might wake up from a coma is totally relevant," Susan said.

"Nothing is certain, Susan, especially not these day. I just hope that it is not true, that everyone I touch with my love, dies," James replied.

"Don't believe in that Black Diamond curse, Sir. Things just happen cause of the times we live in," John said.

"This is exactly why we are planning a strategy, so we can optimize as best as we can and avoid unnecessary tragedy. We will work at being the best we can be. What happens to Christina and Mathew are very relevant, especially to this meeting. We must decide how we can be the most help. These tariffs, the avoidance of income tax, the lack of economic assistance to the destitute, or any other topic which could inflame passions and diverse attention from the very important topic at hand will not be tolerated," Mayor Stern said, as he tapped his gavel on his desk.

"Doctor Knight is certain that sooner or later Christina will wake up. Whether Mathew will be there by her side when she does wake up, is doubtful," James said.

"But sir, we are just discussing the world we are living in. In every war, there are winners and losers, and Mathew must have seen both sides of the equation while flyking around. The winners call the losers deranged because the losers will be left helpless and powerless and maybe even have a panic attack in public. Other losers, more docile looking, will be sitting on park benches, our park benches; some of them could be ticking time bombs. In this New World, there are far too many migrants wandering around displaced and appearing to be lost and some appear very angry. So we have decided that we are going to arrest the most unpleasant looking, and if they can't afford bail, they will just stay locked up and out of sight," John said.

"People who can't afford homes are in a terrible situation. You arrest them for being homeless, who will be next?" Susan asked.

"How can we afford to be incarcerating all those people? Pitville is a small town, and most of the mines are closed," Mayor Stern asked.

"The vagrants will be placed on our 'Pay to Stay and Stay to Pay' program. They will pay to stay in prison, and they will stay in prison until they can pay their debt for staying in prison," John said.

"But how can they do that, when they can't pay to have a home, or they wouldn't be a vagrant to start with?" Susan asked.

"Once they go to trial, finish serving their sentence, they must pay for their prison stay, no excuse will be tolerated.

We have hired a private collection agency, which will be tracking down all debtors and then re-arrest them. The prison will be their home until their debt to stay is paid, and the whole process will be very economical. We solve the vagrancy problem and the inmates will learn the skill required to do the unskilled labor to keep the prison functional and running in tip-top shape," John said.

"The 'Pay to Stay and Stay to Pay' program sounds like double talk for paying your debt to society not just twice, but for life. The vagrant goes to prison to pay their debt for being vagrant, and then he has to pay to stay in the prison, which imprisons him, until he pays his debt. How can a person argue against this, without sounding ridiculously ironic?" Susan asked.

"The law is the law, and President Peel endorses this law, full heartedly," John said.

"We get so used to seeing destitute people, we forget how horrible it really is to be homeless. I don't blame the losers who go through life pleading for consideration, they really need some," Susan said.

"And I don't blame the winners who are willing to fight to the death for this New World Order," John said.

"John, whose side are you on? What happens if President Peel imprisons all of us? What happens if he walls us all in? Whose side would you be on then, John?" James asked.

"Yours, sir. I would always be on your side. How could a president imprison an entire nation, Sir? And why would he want to?" John said.

"A power drunk doesn't give up his power, the withdrawal will hurt too much," Susan said.

"I hope you will always remember that, John. When you wonder which loyalties matter most, remember whose side you are on. What happens if one day, we wake up and find ourselves walled in, as if we were in a prison? Who will help you escape, Peel or me?" James asked.

"That is impossible sir, how could one man enslave an entire territory? Anyway our constitution is designed to prevent tyrants, not to allow them to imprison us," John said.

"Mass dependency on one-man personality cult is how tyrants are made. It is not how great nations are built. We are being weakened and walled in by travel bans, tariffs and walls. I don't blame anyone for wanting to be on the winning side, but I do blame people getting fooled by a one-man personality cult and a lot of smoke and mirrors. Mathew loved taking pictures of contrasts. He used to focus on the gaps between people and the differences between the rich and poor. These differences used to jump out at you in his photographs. Winning is not easy, but losing looks so pathetic, especially in black and white. Just look at all those losers out there in the cold. They should remind us all, how easy it is to fail. The life transforming issue is always the same, one side loses big so the other side can win big. Big winners don't win through kindness and negotiation. Small winners win that way. Small winners take the time to be nice, but look where it gets them," James said.

"Nowhere," John said.

"Exactly, John, the biggest winners don't need to be nice to win," James said.

"Exactly Mr. Coaltonstone and this is the New World Order we must be showing our patriotism too. Big winners fight to the death to win. That is why the Brotherhood and the New World Order is going to win," John said.

"How can anyone think that they have won, when they are killed as they try to be the biggest winner of all?" Susan asked.

"Big winners win by creating huge losses for the opposition. Big winners take everything they can for themselves. I blame those who stay silent and polite, while we are being walled in, soon there will be fences and no-entry signs built around us. They think being nice in this doggy eat dog world works. The big winners know better," James said.

"You can say that again, Mr. Coaltonstone," John said.

"You can see why Mathew enjoyed flyking in the sky as much as he did. There are so many things going on these days that are either alienating, stressful or just too dammed depressing for one's own good. It must be super peaceful flyking up there, in the sky, with the birds and the clouds, well maybe not the clouds. There are some pretty ferocious looking clouds up there these days. Some of those clouds are so charged up, they almost seem unnatural," Susan said.

"Susan, it is amazing. It makes you feel like a kid again," James said,

"Mr. Coaltonstone you know you are not supposed to be flyking. Your life insurance won't be covering you if you get hurt. And you know how those black clouds really scare me and should be scaring you. They always seem to be in a super charged up state," Susan said.

"I know Susan, but it doesn't change the fact that I find flyking very enjoyable. Those black clouds really do scare me. Sometimes I wonder if those clouds are being weaponized," James said.

"I just hope if someone is weaponizing those clouds, that they are on our side," John said.

"I actually have been talking to Doctor Knight. She keeps me informed in matters concerning Mathew's mother and little James. When Christina wakes up, Doctor Ashley said that she will need a purpose, a reason to stay awake, something to live for. Doctor Knight fears that if Christina finds out that Mathew has been shot and is missing, she may not know how to cope, and will relapse" James said.

"Losing kids in this time of war is not that unusual any more. People have to find ways to cope because the enemy wants us to feel deranged and displaced," John said.

"For hundreds, if not thousands of years, boys close to Mathew's age die in wars that a bunch of old men start. The old men will never meet the young men. It is like they are living in worlds that are engineered to be separate by projecting and maintaining their parallel worldviews. When the two worlds do meet, they tend to clash in a power struggle, as if the clash were a foregone conclusion. When the young men are killed in war, the old men might put the young men's names up on a wall, and show them some respect for that moment. Soon the old men go on with their lives with few interruptions returning to their parallel universe," Susan said.

"What the hell are you talking about, Susan?" John asked.

"All I am saying is that Mathew's situation needs to be put into the context of the world that we are now living in. And if you are following President Peel's tweets, which you obviously are doing at this very moment, you must feel the darkness too. We are being pulled back in time. If the End Days have not arrived, they soon may," Susan said.

"When Christina wakes up and finds out what happened to Mathew, she will be heart broken," James said.

"Sir, we don't know what happened to Mathew," John said.

"That is why we need to put this situation in context with what is happening to other young men, so Christina and the rest of us, don't feel so alone in our grief," Susan said.

"Mr. Coaltonstone, do you really think Christina will wake up, soon?" Susan asked.

"Absolutely! Doctor Knight is certain that all she needs is time. Doctor Knight is also very optimistic that little James will continue to thrive," James said as the look on his face betrayed the doubt that he was actually feeling.

"You are looking really doubtful, Sir," Susan said.

"Susan," John scolded.

"There was something that Doctor Knight said that was worrisome. She said that she sees light sometimes in the sky very close to our ship. She also said sometimes she can hear strange noises, possibly the same noises Christina heard before she fell off the ship," James said.

"That sounds very suspicious to me, Sir. There are UFO sightings all the time around that location," Susan said.

"The boots on the ground have been ordered to only report the sightings to the higher-ups, orally. It is all very hush, hush. No paper trail of any kind. And that is all I am authorized to say, Sir," John said.

"Why be so secretive? If there is any danger to Christina, to my ship or to Doctor Knight, I need to know, John. It is the only decent way to handle such events, is to share information. If the information can't be made public, at least allow the people closest to the danger know what is going on so they are able to manage the risks," James said.

"Sir, the problem is, we don't know what is going on, and that is part of the secret. Another part of the secret is that we use very big words and a lot of code words. Words civilians won't understand the meaning of, Sir," John said.

"You mean double talk?" Susan asked.

"Susan," Mayor Stern scolded.

"We are supposed to be knowledgeable of all things going on, even when some of those things have no known explanation. No one in this room is allowed to repeat this information or lack of information to anyone, since it is classified. There are many things that Jethro and Bill are not authorized to tell us," John explained.

"How can we plan a search for Mathew, if we are not allowed to know anything? It doesn't really matter what Jethro and Bill say sir, few people expect to hear the truth from them anymore," Susan replied.

"The point being, Susan, life is full of pitfalls, and the toughest people get that way by picking themselves up after they are kicked down," Mayor Stern said.

"You can say that again, Sir," Susan said.

"Once a person is back on his or her feet again, they need to confront the forces that turned their lives upside down," Mayor Stern said.

"What happens if those forces don't exist, officially?" Susan asked.

"You still have to believe what you believe, or you will be driven crazy," Mayor Stern said.

"That is exactly why we get political," Susan replied.

"The problem is, sir, we don't know what a UFO is. And that is classified information. I must repeat, no word of this part of the conversation is allowed to leave this room," John said.

"I find all this quite unbelievable. Nevertheless, Mathew has been mistaken for a UFO and shot down. Would we even be allowed to know, if the ministry knew what the UFOs are, John? James asked.

"No Sir, you would not be informed. What we do know is that Jethro and Bill made a huge mistake when one of them shot down Mathew. As head of security for the Big Seven Coal Group and a respected member of the security community in general, I am privy that there are letters and reports classified as 'MOST SECRET'. These letters and reports quietly make the rounds and are usually UFO related," John said.

"Are those classifications intentionally hiding information from the general public about UFOs?" Mayor Stern asked.

"More correctly, Sir, I think those letters are hiding what the government doesn't know. I know these documents exist, but I haven't actually been given access to any of them," John explained.

"If UFOs exist..." Susan started to say.

"Actually we know we are getting sightings of UFOs, we just don't know what they are, that is why they are being called Unidentified Flying Objects, Susan," John explained.

"Let's say the UFOs are from out of space, why are they being treated like they are bad, they possibly could be very nice," Susan said.

"Probably only if they are trying to sell us something," James interjected.

"If these UFOs are from out of space, and land without proper documentation they are technically illegal aliens," John said.

"You are kidding, John, right?" Susan asked.

"I don't think John looks like he is kidding, Susan. John, put down your phone and pay attention to our meeting," James demanded as he noted John's steely look.

"A.B. Peel is tweeting about the illegals and vagrants again. He is also tweeting out against the people who are publicly criticizing his Exclusion League backers," John said.

"John, as head of security, you must be paying attention to what is going on here," James interjected.

"I know there are a lot of community groups that have filed requests under the Privacy Act, for access to documents relating to UFO sightings and missing persons' reports, all for naught. Apparently full disclosure, and government by the people, for the people doesn't include sharing UFO sightings or making them public to the people," Susan complained.

"We have stealth planes and stealth drones that are able to defy regulations especially in wartime, who says our enemy states can't do the same? James Coaltonstone asked.

"Exactly, Mr. Coaltonstone, the government is assuming the UFOs are some kind of experimental military aircraft, from the other side," John said.

"The hackers are stealing and selling our stealth technology to the Minese government which makes maintaining national security even more complicated than it already is," John said.

"But kids like Mathew can be detected through radar when they are flyking in the skies as casually as a kid may have biked on a city street only a few years ago. The world has gone crazy. There is no rhyme or reason to anything anymore," James said.

"Sir, Mathew was living his dream. There was nothing he preferred to do than flyke in the open sky," Susan said.

"Sadly, the sky is not open during wartime, Susan, and Mathew was mistaken for an unidentified flying object or some form of enemy drone, because we are living in terrible state of affairs. Our people who are wearing the boots on the ground, so to speak, have to be objective when they shoot to kill. And to be honest, Sir, flyking above a war zone was a reckless endangerment of Mathew's own life. Casualties of war happen all the time," John said.

"This isn't the first time that the militia shot at something in the air, without really knowing what it was they were shooting at," Susan said.

"Susan, any sighting of an unidentified flying object will be classified as ''MOST SECRET','' John said.

"Yes, I know, but how many times has the militia used deadly force, shooting into the sky, and then in the morning we find local towns devastated by our own friendly fire, claiming that they were shooting at UFOs?" Susan asked.

"There are no statistics, for good reason. That information is classified 'MOST SECRET', Susan. You know that we are just following the rules. We all know that we must follow the rules at all times," John said.

"We are getting a lot of complaints from civilians. Cars are ruined. Rooftops have been set on fire and now Mathew has been shot down. Our troops say they are shooting at UFOs but they sure are leaving our side looking like a war zone. Strangely, none of our planes are being shot down. None of our troops are being shot. Whatever unidentified flying object our side is shooting at in the sky, it is not returning fire or dropping bombs on us either," Mayor Stern said.

"And that God for that," John said.

"Susan could you meet me in my office in a couple of hours. I want to dictate a letter outlining my concerns to the Ministry of War, concerning this random destruction, by the ministry," Mayor Stern added.

"Certainly Sir, this kind of tragedy hurts those closest to the victims, for everyone else life goes on as if nothing ever happened," Susan said, as she tidied around her computer, speaking in a practiced tone typical of those who tread on eggshells for a living, all day long.

"It would have killed Mathew to be forbidden to flyke. Mathew lived life as if his life were his own. It was his life. He loved flyking and taking photographs and feeding the wildlife part of his lunch. He always said he could feel his dad's presence the most when he was flyking in the heavens," James said.

"The most important question we should be asking is 'what can we do to find out what really happened to Mathew'?" Mayor Stern said. "I am the elected authority around here. I am the Mayor and the only one who officially is allowed to delegate power to others."

"So why can't you order Jethro and Bill to tell you what happened to Mathew?" Susan asked.

"Susan, why can't you just do your job and take notes? Mayor Stern asked.

"Because all this suffering caused by one disaster after another is distracting me and making me feel super agitated. I also feel that it is morally repugnant to stay silent while Jethro and Bill appear to be getting away with murder. I am sorry, Sir. I miss and Ginger a lot, too. And Maria is just heart broken. Christina would be too if she were awake," Susan said, as she apologized out of necessity.

"Careful, Susan, you are treading on dangerous ground. You know what the militia does do traitors in wartime? They tie their hands behind their backs, then they put a rubber tire over their head and force it down over their shoulders, and then they pour gasoline over them, and light them on fire. And don't think they will spare you because you are a woman. Some of them call themselves feminists too. If you manage to survive their wrath, you might land up suffering from a lifetime of stress induced psychosis. You could be haunted by voices that never stop speaking and yelling at you," John said.

"The only voice I can hear right this minute, is yours, and I wish I could make it stop, but I can't," Susan said.

"Susan and John, please," Mayor Stern scolded.

"John, what you just described doesn't sound legal," James said in protest.

"Since when being a traitor was legal? We take it very seriously," John replied.

"It can be argued that when we have a president who is acting insane, and betraying our constitution, doing nothing, is treason," James said.

"There is our side and the enemy side. And helping the enemy is treason. Whose side are you on, Mr. Coaltonstone?"

"In wartime, sides are blurred, even more so than during peacetime," James said.

"John, what you said sounds very threatening and horrible," Susan said as she started to cry.

"This meeting is getting out of order. So where was I?" Mayor Stern asked, as he pushed a box of Kleenex towards Susan and banged the table with his official gavel so hard that it broke in two.

"My God, are you okay, Mr. Stern?" Susan asked as she blew her nose.

"That was my only gavel," Mayor Stern said as he looked at the broken piece lying on the floor.

"Sir, would you like to borrow mine?" John offered.

"What are you doing with a gavel?" Susan asked.

"You never know when you might need one to show who is boss around here," John said as he gave Susan a penetrating glare.

"Thank you John. I will keep this one if you don't mind, until I can get a replacement," Mayor Stern said.

"Certainly, Sir, I have several more at home," John said as Susan stared at him in disbelief.

"Please people, let us have some order," Mayor Stern said as he tapped his desk with John's gavel. "I remember now. We are around this table because, okay, I am sitting at this table because I am the only legitimate power at this table, in charge of Pitville. We, as human beings are given a great gift, which is life. And during our lifetime, we have this threat that continues to lord over us every day of our lives, and that threat is our mortality. Every day we wall ourselves in, use zero tolerance policies and loss prevention policies, so we can feel safer, but we never do. We just grow more rigid and become prisoners in our strict ways of doing things."

"Or in this case, we might become President Peel's prisoners," James said as he agreed with Mayor Stern.

"We never try to get to know each other, or be kinder to each. We make all these laws and bylaws, assuming that we are minimizing the risks that we fear could take over our time and lives. Sadly our alienation, from each other and ourselves, just grows. When we find people that have fallen through the cracks we force them into some form of incarceration, which now includes the 'Pay to Stay and Stay to Pay' clause, and call it rehabilitation. And then we send them back out again to an even worse situation than the one they were taken from, without any integration, without any job certainty and without even a home. The more alienated we grow to be, the more we want to control the laws that rule nature and ourselves. The predators eat the creatures beneath them, but the creatures beneath do not eat the predators, they run away from them. As I sit in this room, I am asking, no I am demanding that every single one of you elevate yourselves beyond the food chain politics that is dominating, not just Pitville, not just our Tut territory, but the entire world," Mayor Stern said. "We must learn to be less ruthless if we all want to get along."

"Mathew lost his father at a very young age, his mother is in a coma, and his half-brother is on life support, what else did that kid have to lose? Not much, did he? He was too young to really take his mortality seriously and he chose to flyke in the heavens above. Mathew chose to feel free as he flyked with the birds. In a big way, Mathew elevated himself to freedom, because he didn't have much left to lose," Susan said.

"Exactly, Mathew spent his time gliding in the space which surrounds us, outside our walls, and he found happiness and beauty there. The biggest mistake that newbies do in business is they have to control everything, inside their walls, and they never look out, until conflicts grow out of control. They don't realize that being authoritarian and depending on a militarized command center to protect markets, stunts growth. How can you find or create new markets if you are afraid of getting to the next level which would mean giving up some control to others. And by others, I don't mean adversaries. I mean people that have mutual benefits to work together on the same goal. People who are demoralized don't even want to go out and do things, let alone establish new markets. Newbies, who make these mistakes alienate so many people around them, they are continually putting out fires, and have little time to even consider the actual market outside their walls. The biggest mistake newbies do in business and in war, is that they let themselves be blinded by their own hypocrisies," James said.

"Sir? What does this have to do with the topic at hand? Are you well, Sir?" John asked.

"Please, don't patronize me, son. The Exclusion League is going to do more damage to our community and our economy than you could possibly imagine. These tariffs are assassinating my markets, and pushing me backwards. I depend on the Minese to maintain my competitive advantage, and I will be dammed if I demand them to wear an 'M' on their left breast. What kind of leader would do that? A failed leader," James said.

"History proves that silence is complicit to tyranny," Susan said.

"Why do you think public corporations will no longer have to file quarterly financial reports? Obviously participating in full disclosure during a time when hyperinflation is making the price of ordinary goods out of reach for ordinary people. Quarterly reports could shine some light on the 'true risk' for shareholders investing in this toxic and volatile market," Susan said.

"But noise is also complicit to tyranny. President Peel's tweets are shocking the public into submission. People are scared that if they criticize President Peel, he will tweet out embarrassing tweets about them. Or worse, order his cronies and followers to watch not only President Peel's critics nonstop, but their loved ones too, until they are all driven crazy with fear and uncertainty," James said.

"No one wants to be excluded but most people don't care when someone they are competing with, is excluded, as far as I can tell," Susan said.

"So how did A.B. Peel and the Exclusion League get elected? Someone must have voted for them, obviously," John said.

"They promised to do a study on missing people and at the same time they promised to sue any vagrant that spoils public ambience by sitting on a curb or falls asleep on a public bench. They also promised to deport illegal immigrants and separate the children from their parents, and to make their lives as difficult and painful as possible. In wartime, people just get meaner," Susan said.

"I suppose war is often an outshoot resulting from rivalry and the viscous competitive nature of business and state business," James said.

"From my point of view, business is being modeled after many of the events, you find going on, at different levels of the food chain, the political climate is no different. There is one way of thinking dictated down the chain and everyone is expected to go along with it, even when chain of command was never designed to include ordinary people in the process. When you see things from a perspective reflecting one's lower status on the chain, a confrontational and oppositional tone, takes over. Then the tone escalates and you are talked to as if you are the scum of the earth, not as an important part of the human food chain's command system," Susan said.

"Susan!" John shouted.

"Business, in its pure form is about adding perceived value, so technically there are winners on both sides. No one is coercing someone to buy, they exchange voluntarily. And somehow the Exclusion League was able to win by defying the odds against them winning, while appealing to the competitive and elitist nature in man," James said.

"Exactly! Just the way some predators on the food chain disguise themselves, then they pounce before devouring their prey," Susan said.

"War is about winning big and losing big. To win the biggest sum zero game of all, you must destroy the opposition's belief that he can win. Once the opposition gives up and surrenders, the side that didn't give up, wins. And best way do that, is to destroy the opposition's frame of mind and his sense of direction. Destroy everything the opposition knows and understands," James said.

"Shock and awe," John said.

"Exactly, then at the end of all great wars, millions of people on both sides will have been killed off. I suppose that the undocumented cannot be counted in the kill count, so they aren't counted. Business, in its purest form does not promote conflict beyond the competitive kind, but it doesn't step in to help the weak when they are dying off. Soon President Peel will be replacing some of the older soldiers with botguards," James said.

"First they come after the ill and disabled, then they come after the immigrants, then the Exclusion League's drones and G.O.D. bots come after the union leaders, including leaders like George Smoothman and Jay T. Paylor. These two men and their friends, Sam and Kevin Jones have been missing since Christmas. So who will the Exclusion League's drones and G.O.D. bots go after next? Possibly anyone of us. Our silence not only makes us complicit, but it makes us vulnerable. And will 'they' be a human or a robot?" Susan asked."

"Susan, put a sock in it," John commanded.

"Business adds value for whoever is able to buy whatever a business is able to sell. Business contributes to happiness and this happy chain of events is able to spiral, just like all other chain of events are able to do. The greatest chain of events known on this planet is the chain of events that occur on the food chain. We will always be participating on the food chain, in one way or another because we are part of the food chain," James said.

"And those who are first on the food chain live the best. Our position on the food chain is predestined," John said.

"Especially if we force the Minese to wear the M on their left breast so we can identify them and then serve them last," James said we disgust.

"We must stay first to maintain the quality of our lives. No other super power should be allowed to overtake our superior position on the food chain," John said.

"The food chain is everything," Susan said sarcastically.

"What else is there? To maintain our quality of life we put ourselves first, and place the Minese last. We marginalize all the Minese, including the illegals and the vagrants to better our lives. We use their labor, because in the strictest sense, their social vulnerability gives business a competitive advantage. The illegals and the vagrants can't access their social rights, because they don't have any social rights to access. The Exclusion League promised the New Social Order, where we don't pretend we can all be first. For some of us to be first, others have to be last," James said.

"We need to take turns with each other, but not with the Minese, that is how our society operates and that is how the New World Order will operate. When the purging of the illegals and the vagrants, is out in the open, our quality of life can only improve," John said.

"The real question is, will cultivating such uncivility towards the Minese really be good for society? Will being so rude to others be a good example for the children to follow? And who will be next?" Susan asked.

"This is exactly what President Peel and his Exclusion League backers, promised to do if they were elected. There was no discussion of increasing tariffs and causing a trade war, there was no discussion of assassinating my markets and possibly even destroying civilization," James said.

"Why would we want to make life any different for the illegals and the vagrants, and what does this discussion have to do with finding Mathew?" John asked.

"Maybe Jethro and Bill thought Mathew was a vagrant and shot him down, and then later made up a cover-up story. Mr. Coaltonstone, you also have those two men on your payroll that just shot your stepson down from the sky and are now refusing to tell you the truth," Susan suggested.

"And the brotherhood is not allowing me to fire them or I would have by now. We are no longer playing by the rules of civil society. The rules of war are brutal, such rules don't even pretend to be civilized. It is all about natural selection, the best of the best will win. The losers don't matter because they no longer exist," James said.

"So this is the way it should be. We only need winners, we don't losers," John said.

"What a great idea! All the brutes of the world should beat up and kill all the artists and intellectuals of the world, and then we can all evolve into Neanderthals, where silence is only disturbed by grunts. And when our young go missing or are shot down by friendly fire, we just except it as part of what happens now," Susan said.

"Shut up Susan," John ordered.

"Your point, James?" Mayor Stern asked.

"The institution of war is the opposite of the institution of civilization. When we are being civilized, we all matter. The people matter and my stepson matters. When we are operating in the fog of war, all that we hold dear, art, music and beautiful architecture are destroyed. It is always about winning not about living in the Age of Enlightenment or in the Age of Reason. War is about winning, big time. No one wins at war by being reasonable, but you do win at business when being reasonable. Everyone goes into war, assuming they are going to win, but no one goes into war by assuming they have to be reasonable to win. They go into war assuming the most ruthless will win. If anything people go into war because they don't have to be reasonable," James said.

"We are winning, Sir," John interjected.

"What does winning even mean? And John, are you sure that you are on my side? There are wins for the old men who do not fight and just dish out orders. It is their world, they own most of it, but what about 'we, the people'? The constitution was about 'we, the people' and the right to pursue happiness. Not just about the one percent who brainwash us into thinking that life is just another sum zero game that we have to resort to evil tactics to win. War is not a game, son. War is about loss, grief, amputations and death," James started to raise his voice to be heard over Susan's sobs.

"Of course I am on your side, Sir," John said.

"As I said before..." Mayor Stern began to say.

"Ted, I am not finished speaking," James said. "The most important factor in business, is not just the person you are selling to, but the person's imagination, the person's sense of utility and his confidence in his future. Is it necessary to risk that sense of confidence in the future by unilaterally declaring war? Then the other side declares war, in retaliation. The whole situation is stupid, mindless and unnecessary. Now my beautiful stepson has been shot down by friendly fire and we have no idea if he is dead, or alive. How stupid is that? A person, who knows how to sell anything, knows how to inflame a person's passions and could sell war, but why would he? The newbies assume it is just the person in the show room they are selling to, but the buyer is interested in a product because of the value and improvements to his or her life the product will bring. What improvements will war bring? We sit here, and allow this mad man, we call President Peel, to dictate to us that war is good when it is bad and unnecessary. We, the people could lose everything. People buy things to increase performance and increase their attraction. People don't buy things to get killed or to get maimed, so why would they buy war, voluntarily? Because they are being told that they will be winners, which is a lie. No one wins at war except those who are selling the arms of destruction and insanity. It is the same with this newbie Exclusion League government. Once this new administration takes control, our lives could be changed forever. Opportunities and obstacles shape everyday people. When everyday people get the chance to grow, their abilities improve and their opportunities increase. If people get stifled by all the new rules and regulations the newbie government imposes on them, they start to decay and their life tends to fall apart all around them. And only the members of the elite cliques get to benefit from growth and opportunity, but those same cliques will never benefit from the missed opportunities of preventing this war, now will they?" James asked.

"Does it matter?" John asked.

"Of course it matters. Quality of life matters. Quality of mercy matters. My beautiful Bering Strait Hyper-Loop rail Peace Complex matters because it will bring everyone together, and save an incredible amount of money in shipping and travel costs. And it will be fun. Just like John said, it will be like riding inside a roller coaster tube, but with a lot less hills," James said.

"If you can pull it off, Mr. Coaltonstone, we will be creating a new market in travel and transport and we would be living the dream, Sir," John said.

"And new markets will be necessary if President Peel succeeds in assassinating my markets. When we give out positive energy we often get twice as much back and it is the same with negative energy. All I feel when I read President Peel's tweet is gloom and doom. When I work on this project, I start to see the light at the end of the tunnel," James said.

"That is very good, because without that light at the end of the tunnel, my claustrophobia could get out of control if

I were to travel in your new hyper-loop rail service, James, though it sounds very exciting. I just hope we can find Mathew, so he can enjoy it too," Mayor Stern said.

"Talk about missed opportunity. Without opportunity, our range of experience diminishes. With missed opportunities, we will never know who we could have been. When we lack opportunities, and miss opportunities, our minds begin to narrow. Having a chance to grow our skills and wealth is what makes life worth living and increases our depth, as people. And all that was taken from Mathew was also taken from all of us. All of Mathew's potential horizons are now out of reach. Mathew and his freedoms, or lack of them mattered. The future matters. My hyper-loop rail service is the ride into the future. The future that we still have, and Mathew might have lost due Jethro and Bill's stupidity," James said as he banged his coffee cup on the table with a loud thumping sound.

"You mean Mathew matters, not mattered. I really feel that Mathew is somewhere struggling to stay alive. I also believe all that positive energy that Mathew generated will make him stronger, wherever he may be. I know that there is a force out there protecting him. Mathew still time on his side," Susan said.

"I hate to interrupt this conversation which is very interesting but I must remind you all, that I am the only democratically elected official sitting at this table," Mayor Stern said. "In theory, I am the only legitimate power sitting in the red chair at the head of this table. Every other power struggle that goes on in this room or anywhere else is either between shadow people, or shadow government or deep shadow government. Ever since the City Hall was burnt to the ground after you shot Ginger Goodwin, John, we have been stuck in these temporary offices, but we are technically still sitting in a Pitville city hall meeting, and the meeting should still be in order, until I say otherwise. I have no time for anything else but official government business, no time whatsoever. Am I making myself clear? Bill and Jethro do not have the power or the right to kill indiscriminately. And neither do you, John Bell. The Pitville taxpayers will demand an explanation for this reckless behavior by two government officials who either murdered a child or endangered a child. A child was possibly killed for no good reason, because two fools, armed to the teeth, assumed that he was an unidentified flying object."

"Sir, G.O.D. declared that I had every right to shoot Ginger Goodwin, because it was in self-defense. I feel terrible about what happened to our beautiful city hall, but we are making do. This is wartime. People die, buildings are destroyed. It is true that you are the elected mayor of Pitville and we are your support staff. You can't be in charge all alone, Sir, when the Social Problem is so out of hand, you need us to help you to maintain order," John Bell said.

"No, John, I am not just in charge of Pitville, I represent the people of Pitville and I run Pitville. When I demand silence, I expect silence," Mayor Stern interjected as he glanced at James hoping to get a signal that he was agreeing with him and that James had his back.

"Of course you run Pitville, Ted," James said agreeably while winking knowingly at John.

"This is wartime, Sir. People lose everything in wartime. There are a lot of broken people sitting on curbs all day long doing nothing and during the night they sleep on park benches. Sometimes they are recruited to pick fruit, but these days the chain gangs or illegals do that kind of work. If they wake up the next morning, they remain idle, doing nothing all day but sitting on a curb rotting, hunting for food and a place to go to the bathroom. That is the way it is now for a lot of people in Pitville, Sir," John said.

"John, let's talk about this later, over drinks, my treat. Susan hand me your notes," Mayor Stern ordered. Mayor Stern quickly shredded the notes. "I will dictate official minutes of this meeting to one of the girls from the secretarial pool. We don't need to be taking notes about our discussion about

UFOs. It sounds too crazy. We all have a reputation to keep. Do you have anything else you want to say, Susan, before you are excused from this meeting?" Mayor Stern said.

"Yes, Sir. Time runs everything, Trying to control all life is futile," Susan said as Mayor Stern looked at his watch.

"We are getting way behind and before you know it, the day will be over, and nothing has really changed," Susan said.

"As we speak my tunnels are being bored, capsules are being manufactured and my hyper-loop train is being built. I wish Mathew were here to enjoy all this. President Peel and his war mongering is ruining everything way beyond what Peel is even aware of," James said.

"Time is setting on Mathew's destiny," Susan said.

"Susan, shut up, if you can't just do your job and take notes go home," John said without giving Susan any eye to eye contact.

"We can't just let the militia riff-raff and glorified spies take over and kill our children as if they were nothing more than just tragic collateral damage," Susan said as she rose up from her seat to leave the room, James held her back.

"Come on you guys, Susan stay, we can work this out. That is what politics is all about. War is different than politics, or at least, it should be. We are better off being honest with each other. The worse thing about spies, the ones not on our side, they lie to us, and they convince us to make decisions that are not in our best interest," James said. "This meeting was supposed to be about Mathew, and Mathew was very dear to me. He was my stepson, but I wonder whose side President Peel is really on. While the president is walling us in, we are turning on each other, without realizing why. Our children are getting shot down by people who are supposed to be on our side."

"So should we assume that Mathew is dead or should we hope that he is just another missing person, another casualty of war?" John asked.

"John, please," James pleaded, as he sounded weak and frail, which startled the others sitting around the table.

"James are you okay?"

"I am fine. I am just with Susan on this. I feel that Mathew is alive too. Blood found at the shooting scene would indicate that he is injured, and he needs our help. We need to keep our minds focused on our objective, which is to find Mathew and bring him home, before Christina wakes up.

"Strangely, I am agreeing with Mr. Coaltonstone," Susan said.

"Who are you, Susan? You don't make any decisions, and your opinions are stupid and childlike," John said in his usual condescending tone.

"I have a feeling, just like Mr. Coaltonstone does, that Mathew is still alive and needs our help. If we assume he is dead and give up on our search and rescue mission, we fail Mathew," Susan said.

"Susan has a point, we need to give Mathew a fighting chance and not assume that he is dead. We must work as a team and strengthen our resolve and try to find Mathew and bring him home. We can't give up, before we try to find him," James said.

"We can't assume that the impact of the shooting killed Mathew. We don't know for sure if Mathew is dead or alive. We should continue our mission as if it is a rescue mission, until evidence proves otherwise," John said.

"Exactly! The search and rescue team only found feathers and a bit of blood, so we should assume Mathew is missing and continue searching," Susan said. "Jethro and Bill are confusing the issue the way they did when the whale was blown up. Jethro is blaming Bill, and Bill is blaming Jethro. Even the news is getting the story mixed up which will prejudice the case if it ever gets to court, which I have my doubts. In some online publications it is Jethro who killed the whale. Maria believes that Jethro killed the whale and shot Mathew down. Lots of people think that both men, Jethro and Bill, are out of control. No one likes being spied on and no one likes children being shot out of the sky as if they were nothing but an unidentified flying object," Susan said.

"I didn't know you knew Maria," James said.

"We talk sometimes. After Mathew's dad was killed, Maria kept to herself. Then by coincidence we found ourselves taking the same etherplayer music class and got to know each other better,"

"Etherplayer music class?" James asked. "Isn't that the instrument people play without touching it? Something to do with creating good harmonic vibes from the Ether Region?"

"More importantly, it is about bonding with the Ether Music, sir," Susan explained.

"We need to get back to Mathew Junior, Sir. Time is not on his side. If he is hurt, he will need our help. If he has been kidnapped or taken prisoner he will need our help. And if he is dead, we will need to file a request to submit a death certificate," John said.

"What happens if we never get closure, never find the truth? Never find Mathew?" James asked.

"Jethro and Bill seem to be going out of their way to mix everything and everyone up. We have no idea what really happened. At the moment, they don't seem to be accountable to anyone. They don't seem to have an overseer of any kind. Do those botcops and dronecops ever watch them the way they watch us?" Susan asked.

"Speak for yourself Susan, no botcop supervises or watches me," James said.

"Are you sure, Mr. Coaltonstone?" Susan asked.

"One hundred percent positive. We may have walls and barbed wire surrounding us, but it does not change who we are. I am James Coaltonstone. The botcops may be watching me but they cannot supervise me. They do not have the authority to be abusing their authority. At least, not yet, anyway. I am in charge of my own destiny and I do not allow those botcops inside my head. I supervise myself. However, I do agree with your sentiment, Susan," James said.

"Those fools, Jethro and Bill have way too much power for their own good as well as for everyone else's good," Susan said.

"Jethro and Bill have a much higher security clearance than you ever will, Susan. And may I add, your pay scale does not justify all the time you take up talking," John said.

"As pay scales go, I am better value because I don't go around blowing up whales that are swimming in the sea and I am not shooting down children who are flyking in the sky. After blowing up a whale and shooting down Mathew, Jethro and Bill should be fired, with no pay. And I won't even mention how I feel about Jethro and Bill's high security clearance. It is frightening that they are still floating around in that nuclear sub, as if nothing has happened. It is very demoralizing and it is a travesty of justice," Susan said.

"I hate to admit it but Susan is right, even Maria swears that it was Jethro that blew up the whale and bullied Bill to take the blame. I wish I never hired those two," James said as his voice cracked a little.

"Sir, Bill said that he was the one who blew up the whale because Jethro told him to," John interjected. "Jethro admitted to shooting Mathew. I believe that," John said.

"Does it even matter what happened as much as what will happen again, if we choose to do nothing?" Susan asked while looking at John.

"We all have to follow procedure and rules which includes documenting any evidence that we find, regardless of whose side we are on, before we assume guilt," John said.

"The truth is partly what is known and partly what is unknown, so opinions and memories differ between people and everyone starts to argue assuming the other person is wrong instead of just experiencing another part of the same puzzle. When everyone is arguing it makes it even harder to remember what happened. We are always facing that dilemma all the time in politics," Mayor Stern said. "The one who gets it wins, regardless of all the fog in the battlefield."

"For Mathew's sake we need to at least be on the right path. And when the path comes to an intersection, we must make sure that we don't make a wrong turn," Bob said.

"Or crash into something," Susan added.

"How can we follow rules that seem to be designed to distract us from knowing which path to take?" James asked.

The League's investigation must be based on evidence because both Jethro and Bill have rights," John Bell explained.

"And they are stalling while time is setting on Mathew and his destiny. I mean as far as we know those two could have sold him into slavery while milking him for his young blood," Susan interjected.

John over-explained. "It is obvious that Jethro and Bill are hiding something because they are protecting their asses, nevertheless we must follow the rules and procedures. Or..."

"Or what?" Susan asked.

"I don't want to alarm anyone, but Jethro and Bill are authorized to shoot us too," John said.

"Don't be so melodramatic," Mayor Stern ordered.

"With all respect Sir, we are at war and we are under martial law and the Social Problem must be solved," John replied. "I cannot stress enough that we remain vigilant. We often make split second life and death decisions, if we don't shoot fast enough, we are shot at. Jethro and Bill feel the same threat and have the same mindset. Any generated data from G.O.D.'s bothead related to Jethro and Bill's data can be changed, adjusted and omitted. Any involuntary input, created under duress and coercion is considered off limits to our investigation, Sir."

"So what kind of protocol does that imply, John?" James asked.

"Deadly, sir. Voluntary means what voluntary, like the way the word always has. Lots of words used these days often have the opposite meaning to what we are used to the word meaning," John replied.

"So, John you are coming over onto my side?" Sue asked.

"Susan, we were always on the same side" John said. "Bill and Jethro keep changing their stories so we no long believe a word they say, which poses a nightmare security risk for our team, Sir," John added.

"And the Brotherhood won`t let me fire them," James said.

"As far as we can tell from the evidence we have at present, Sir, Bill and Jethro's intentions were noble when they shot Mathew down. It was the information they had that was at fault. The database they were using had many data points that were faulty, and were not verifiable due to secrecy laws, Sir. From their point of view, Sir, Mathew was just one more unidentified flying object roaming around in a cluttered sky, during wartime, protected by secrecy laws, Sir," John explained.

"Does that even make sense, John?" James asked.

"In this day and age Sir, it does, Sir, it really does," John said.

"This is all very worrisome, and very tragic," Mayor Stern said.

"Jethro and Bill have always been worrisome. I hired those two to improve my security, and ever since they have been on my payroll I have never felt so insecure in my life," James said as he sipped from the flask that was no longer hidden in his coat pocket. And I can't fire them," James interjected.

"Why can't you fire Jethro and Bill, James?" Mayor Stern asked.

"Because they belong to the Brotherhood, Sir," John interrupted.

"No wonder so many people are saying that we are at the dawning on the post-human age," Susan said.

"Again, I agree with Susan. I tried to get more information from Jethro and Bill too, but all I got back was an email referring my office to their lawyer who is being funded by the G.O.D bank."

"Who is their lawyer?" James Coaltonstone asked.

"Muni Bugden," John Bell replied.

"Christina's old lawyer," James noted.

"What side is that guy on?" Susan asked.

"Susan!" Mayor Stern shouted. "Your job is to take notes, not ask questions," Mayor Stern scolded.

"I guess he goes where the money is," Susan added.

"Actually, Muni Bugden is representing the Brotherhood because he always has. Both Jethro and Bill are lifelong members of the Brotherhood and many of the members love Jethro and Bill like brothers," John explained.

"Figures," Susan interjected.

"Susan!" Mayor Stern shouted again.

"This time I am tending to agree with Susan," John said.

"This meeting is not about Muni Bugden, this meeting is about finding out what happened to my stepson," James said.

"Of course sir," John replied.

"Do you think we will ever find out what really happened to Mathew? Everywhere we turn we get stonewalled. I just want Mathew back," James Coaltonstone said as he began to sob.

"Sir you must eat, you are our leader," Susan said as she placed a glass of red wine and a hardboiled egg in front of James Coaltonstone.

"I miss Mathew's laughter, our talks, our flyking outings," James said in between sobs.

"Sir, you know you are not allowed to flyke, your life insurance policy forbids it," Susan said before both Mayor Stern and John Bell shouted "Susan shut up," at the same time.

CHAPTER 2:

Two Races: The Minese and the Buynese

March 17th 2031, around 4:00 PM: "What do you mean the Exclusion League is declaring that Mary and David are not the same race as we are? Does that mean that they won't be able to shop in the same places that we do? Why do these people make everything so hard?" Dianne Black, PPZ newscaster and social media personality asked while covering her phone, just before she hung up in frustration.

"I really need a break from talking to that G.O.D. bot, but I want to make this adoption work, so much. David and Mary need, us," Dianne said.

"And we need them, family is everything. Family helps make this crazy world easier to take," Jackson said.

"Only the Exclusion League backers would delegate the authority to G.O.D. bots to perform as social workers in wartime to save money," Dianne said.

"It is crazy, the entire world has gone crazy," Jackson said.

"How can it be even determined who is a pure Minese and who is a pure Buynese? Dianne asked.

"The Minese will have to wear the letter 'M' on their left breast, I guess that is the only way. That is part of President Peel's tweet of the day. In truth I really don't know how a person can tell the Minese from the Buynese, otherwise," Jackson said.

"President Peel's tweets are hardening public opinion, I mean big time. So many people I know, decent people who aren't prejudice most of the time, follow every word that demagogue tweets, and the words start to take over their minds," Dianne said.

"His logic is oxymoronic, which is why I think President Peel doesn't have a clue. I also think he is intentionally manipulating his followers, big time. The sheer brutality of his daily thoughts, when tweeted out, makes great tweets but terrible government policy, especially because they don't just shock, but awe people. If his tweets were just a joke and not for real, it wouldn't be so bad, but he is turning his tweets into public policy, which is scary. And I really doubt that all the Minese people staying under the Tut territory will be wearing the M, voluntarily. The Minese will just have to be more careful, more secretive and more segregated from the rest of us, to maintain their sense of dignity and self," Jackson said.

"Hard to imagine things getting worse for them. They are being forbidden to shop in the same stores that we shop in. Next thing you know, President Peel will be sending out G.O.D. bots to take away the young Minese to an unknown location for an unknown purpose. If one side of the family lives or works underground and the other side of the family lives and works above ground, who really is a pure Minese? Will the mixed population also have to wear the M'? " Jackson asked.

"Why do they have to make things so hard for us and the kids?" Dianne asked.

"I really don't know, Di. Maybe President Peel doesn't know why he is making things so hard for us either," Jackson replied.

"I bet he does. The Exclusion League believes that the natural way of things is that there will always be scarcity. You know what I mean. That doggie eat dog, G.O.D.'s way or no way if not our way, mentality. And if you don't like it just go away," Dianne said.

"I really do think President Peel doesn't have a clue. I really think that he doesn't get it that part of the natural scarcity that he believes in so much, is due to the hoarding and mismanagement of the surplus. It is his greed that is causing scarcity. Day after day they waste so much. They waste resources, and incredible amounts of time," Jackson said.

"It is just mind boggling how much time he is wasting with all those crazy tweets," Dianne said.

"That is exactly what I am saying. A man in Peel's position doesn't waste his time. I think that Peel's strategy is to make people feel like insiders, in the same way that new shoot shoot-em-up phone-game does. Those kids want to belong so much, they want to be part of the in-crowd, which makes those kids exceptionally vulnerable. The phone-game, they are playing starts with people waiting in the park. The kids spend time looking around, because everyone is trying to find a way to survive, so they can play the game for longer. And while everyone is trying to find ways to survive, everyone is also getting points whenever they kill someone," Jackson said.

"Sounds like our war with Mina," Dianne said.

"Exactly, and while the kids are playing this phone-game they can be located through their phones, and now a mass kidnapper-murderer, or a group of them, sometimes they kidnap these kids and sometimes they just shoot them, in broad daylight," Jackson explained.

"Wow, why can't the kids stop playing, and why aren't the authorities doing something to stop this madness?" Dianne asked.

"I don't know if the authorities are investigating or not. Usually such investigations lead to posters and lengthy reports and not much else happens. The kids are being told the kidnappings and murders have nothing to do with the game, it is just a terrible coincidence that the victims just happen to be playing the game, when they were shot or kidnapped," Jackson said.

"Who produces the game?" Dianne asked.

"A group called the Brotherhood produces the game and they refuse to address the issue or even speak with us. They call us Fake News. I think the kids continue playing the phone-game because the game is exciting, and everyone they know is playing it and they want to belong so much. And in the real world they are treated like outsiders, and they would do almost anything to be part of something bigger than themselves," Jackson said.

"And all that our president seems to do is tweet," Dianne said.

"I don't think President Peel has a clue. Especially when he calls us fake news and the enemy of the people, I think he just doesn't get it," Jackson said.

"I think he does get it. President Peel is on the inside with his cronies, and we are on the outside, like the majority of the public is. That is why we search for the truth and then do our best to report it," Dianne said. "I think he knows if independent journalists dig too deep, they will get inside his card game, and the whole house of cards will come falling down on him. The president is acting as if he has something to hide, and it is our job to expose it all for what it is, and damn all those smoke and mirrors that he uses to confuse everyone."

"I think you are partly right, I also think President Peel doesn't read much, and he has a very narrow scope of insight," Jackson said.

"You can say that again. President Peel is the most narrow-minded person I have ever met and he does nothing to widen the scope of his vision," Dianne said.

"Very scary to have a visionary leader, as president, with such a narrow scope of vision," Jackson said.

"I'll say and he is changing the very nature of our republic. He does nothing to widen his scope of insight. He doesn't read much, he has few books lying around, but I think it is his that is reading them. His wife is very brainy," Dianne said.

"Yes, I heard that she entered the Tut territory using what is dubbed the 'Machiavelli Visa'. But President Peel insulates himself with all of his insiders, who say 'yes' to everything, or they get the boot, and become an outsider pretty quickly," Jackson said.

"I know, President Peel has cocooned himself from the outside world ever since he was a child. He uses Twitter to make his followers feel that they are insiders. He is mesmerizing people who go for those personality cults. This entire situation is almost as crazy as those kids setting themselves up to get murdered in real life," Dianne said.

"I don't think they are separated. The biggest threat to our sanity is loneliness. My love for you, keeps me sane, Di," Jackson confessed.

"I love you too, Jackson," Dianne replied.

"The entire planet has gone berserk. This is supposed to be the information age, but we have a president who shuns all information that doesn't fit his political motives, sometimes I fear for our safety," Jackson said.

"I do too. I believe it is our duty to inspire the public to stay informed. Information empowers people and it widens the entire universal scope of vision and mass consciousness. Only narrow minded or politically motivated people would not understand how important the freedom of the press actually is. President Peel dictates, because he is autocratic by nature, and part of his dictation are those crazy Twitter broadcasts he does day after day. But those tweets also convince his follower that they too are on the inside, not just passive spectators. People

BLACK CLOUD: The Miner Book 5

play this game not to gain insight but for the feeling that they belong to something greater than themselves," Dianne said.

"Scary how it all starts and ends with all that smoke and mirrors. And sometimes those tweets actually scare me and I can feel my psyche being drained of energy. I just think he dictates because his mindset is so narrow, he can't imagine a better way. Just because President Peel is a dictator, doesn't mean that he knows what he is actually doing. He dictates the first thing that comes to his narrow mind, which obviously doesn't include goodwill," Jackson said.

"You are right. President Peel doesn't read much, except if the article or book is about him. And then he gets really mad at me and at the press in general, because he doesn't like what he reads about himself," Dianne said.

"President Peel doesn't seem to understand that dictating self-fulfilling prophecies is not the only option there is, but the hardships that are being cause, needed to be reported by us, so the public is not left in the dark. There are far better ways to treat people. It is not necessary to force people into slavery and starvation, especially with Lance Diamond's prefabricated vertical farm towers popping up in so many places, stricken by drought," Jackson said.

"You think he would be offering more carrots to people to influence their choices and behavior, instead of using that almighty stick of his. He keeps congratulating himself on how tough he is, but he doesn't realize that he is obviously hard and callous, but he probably isn't very resilient. His outdated ideas may be the only option President Peel can imagine because he is a dictator, and he wants total control, he doesn't allow much input from experts or anyone. We all know there are newer and better ways to do things, so as journalists, it is our duty to question the insanity of this administration," Dianne said.

"But should we be risking our lives? I know, it is really hard to know what side President Peel, is really on, but I don't think he is on ours," Jackson said.

67

"My fear is that President Peel and his Exclusion League backers would eliminate all social mobility and mixing, including freedom of the press, if they could. I think this is what this war is all about, culture control. Manufacturing differences between people, separating people and dividing people will lessen bonds between people so when people are separated, it doesn't hurt as much. Manufacturing our consent to hate and segregate is partly the war psychology growing all around us, but also it is a feeling a lot of people must be enjoying," Dianne said.

"There is a badly kept secret that President Peel is going to be tweeting out the drawing of the military draft lottery," Jackson said.

"I guess it is to show that there is no prejudice when selecting death squads," Dianne said.

"President Peel wants total control because he wants to win big, regardless of who will lose it all. He is just assuming that he will be better off if he dictates by monopolizing life in the Tut territory and keeping all the best stuff for himself and people just like him," Dianne said.

"It is like explaining to a child that sum zero games, are games, but living life like a sum zero game can lead to emptiness and unhappiness. One side wins and one side loses, but in real life it is better not to turn everything into sum zero game, because then everyone is unhappy. The loser is unhappy because he is losing and the winner is unhappy cause in the end the loser stops playing with him," Jackson said.

"President Peel shocks the public into stopping everything they are doing, including driving, just to read his crazy tweets. People are in traffic and they pull over just to read President Peel's tweets. And the big questions are ignored, of course. Is it even legal that President Peel has given himself the authority to manufacture divisions by calling the Minese and the Buynese officially separate races?" Jackson asked.

"Yeah, a war that forbids us from fraternizing with the Minese, conditions the Minese to behave one way and the Buynese another way, and the more separated we are the more culturally divided we grow to be. The Exclusion League knows what they are doing alright," Jackson said.

"And working such long hours without natural light changes people too," Dianne said.

"Yeah, big time. There is almost no better feeling than having the sun shine on your face," Jackson said. "I feel much happier after spending time in the natural light, it is the way love makes a person feel. You feel more open minded, because you just do."

"If only President Peel could just feel some warmth and love for the people he condemns to the margins of society, those people would be better off, but so would he," Dianne said. "This constant hate and disdain for others, might excite some, but still those feelings sooner or later will make them rigid and cold inside. Soon we have little time for those who are different or less successful than we are we close the door on social mobility, very mobility that made Tut so great in the past," Dianne said.

"What are we going to do, Di?" Jackson asked with his eyes fixed on his monitor.

"Simple, we prove that David and Mary have dominant Buynese traits. We prove that the children are more Buynese than they are Minese and that the G.O.D. bots made a computer error," Dianne said.

"Big one is to orient them to being in lighted areas, to enjoy being above ground, and most of all Diane, you want to take them shopping. Teach them how much fun it is to be a mindless consumer," Jackson said.

"Exactly, Mary already loves trying on my shoes and my hats," Dianne said.

"Yes, wait till she sees your pad in the Metropolis," Jackson said.

"Our pad. We have to really act married and live like a couple in love, especially when the social worker bots come and make their official house calls," Dianne said.

"Dianne, I do love you. Sometimes I love you so much it scares me," Jackson said.

"You would not be the first one to say that it takes a brave man to love me. I love you too Jackson and it scares me sometimes," Dianne replied.

"Look at us, two selfless war correspondents, risking our lives to get to the truth by asking difficult questions from some very frightening people, and we are both terrified of love," Jackson said.

"We are not the only ones terrified of love. If we are going to win the battle against President Peel and the Exclusion League, we must stay. We must focus on our plan not on our fear, just the way we do in the battlefield. The assumption is that the Buynese drive the economy, drive the consumer culture and drive the Minese to work like dogs, for very little in return, except for the freedom of being left alone in those horrible, cold, dark tunnels. But technically, the only difference between the Buynese and the Minese are personality traits. Traits that are conditioned in the individual from birth.

It is crazy that G.O.D. bots are even conditioning humans from birth, so they never question what is expected of them, what is appropriate for their class and where they belong and where they don't belong," Dianne replied.

"What about the G.O.D. bots' database documentation system? How do we get around that? Once a person is in the Exclusion League's database as Minese or Buynese that definition defines them for life," Jackson said.

"Ignore it. It is probably classified as 'MOST SECRET' anyway. In the meantime we will try to document David and Mary's link to the Buynese. Most of the Minese work underground and their ancestry often originates from Mina but not all the time. Most of the Buynese work above ground and their ancestry often originated from Buyna, but not all the time either. War with a race, especially a manufactured race, sounds incredibly racist and unconstitutional to me," Dianne said.

"Of course it is. Even for the G.O.D. bots. The directive we received could also be an electro-magnetic interference related computer error," Jackson said.

"Yeah it must be," Dianne said. "We get so many IMIs these days, with all that fake cloud and real cloud extreme weather activity going on. We are at war with the Minese government not the Minese people. These people are just as much victims of politics as we are," Dianne said.

"The world is so crazy and hostile at times. You are either living underground or above ground. No happy medium any more," Jackson said.

"As if the world isn't gloomy enough, why would we need any fake, dark clouds lingering above our heads?" Jackson asked Di.

"Beats me. And those fools, Jethro and Bill, not even considering that there could be kids who are flyking in the open skies. First thing comes to their hot heads are unidentified flying objects. It would be nice to be flyking innocently around, seeing the world before it decays in front of our eyes," Di said.

"What does that President Peel and his crazy Exclusion League expect the result will be from their directive?" Jackson said.

"President Peel calls it Natural Selection, but it really will be Artificial Selection," Dianne replied.

"Global economic growth could come to a stand still and then crash. The resulting benefits would only benefit a small selection of people," Jackson said.

"All those crazy trade tariffs and counter-tariffs are going to get in the way of our friendly M.A.P initiative while opposing sides immerse themselves in enemy market assassinations. Our Mutually Assured Progress could be replaced with Mutually Assured Destruction, and how sad would that be? What kind of leader leads people to self destruction?" Dianne said.

"A lemming? Scary to be pushed back to a time when we had no allies," Jackson said.

"It is an urban myth that lemmings commit mass suicide, but I can't say the same for humans. What is war anyway? I think the Exclusion League backers are expecting to free up assets for the Tut territory once the Minese are killed off, and some of the Exclusion League's non backers go bankrupt. Taking the position that filing quarterly financial reports will no longer be necessary could hide the actual proof that the market is declining into recession, if not depression, and our national currency is being devalued by hyperinflation. Hiding information will allow President Peel to stay willfully blind to the damage these tariffs and counter-tariffs are doing to ordinary people's lives and to the nation's economy. He can continue yelling and screaming at people through his Twitter feed, but where is he truly leading us to?" Dianne said.

"My guess, he is leading us to a place that is super scary," Jackson said.

"Why would President Peel declare a race war and tweet the military draft lotteries if he wasn't preparing for war? Why would he manufacture hardships and social exclusions if he weren't hoping for a reaction? I think he deliberately makes things as hard as he can because he thinks it will be easier for him; a sign of an amateur because he is isolating the entire territory. We are losing our allies and our trading partners are disappearing. The logic is so oxymoronic it makes me want to scream, but I wouldn't want to wake up the children," Dianne said.

"When the Minese are forced to go to inferior stores to shop, it is assumed that is the natural order of things and there will be more of the good stuff left for us. While the Minese are forced to buy food that has gone bad or will go bad soon, President Peel and the Exclusion League backers are assuming that the relationship is naturally adversary. The more rights the

Minese lose the more votes President Peel and the Exclusion League backers seem to win. But in wartime everyone loses," Jackson said.

"How I loathe these G.O.D. bot delegates. It sounds too me this new administration is deliberately trying to fan old flames to keep these manufactured divisions and conflicts escalating."

"It is being assumed that Tut territory will be in control of the pricing and the smaller economies will decay back into their precolonial state," Dianne said.

"President Peel is taking a huge gamble, don't you think, Di?" Jackson asked.

"I'll say, taking care of our new family will do us the world of good. It will be a great escape from all this madness," Dianne said.

"The Social Problem only gets worse when the Exclusion League brings in more promised bureaucracy in the pretense of solving the Social Problem. You really have to be innovative to create new opportunities for people, when there are so few new opportunities left," Jackson said.

"I really feel sorry for Thelma, she gets a lot of hate mail especially when her PPZ weather reports are wrong. The weather is getting harder and harder to predict and they always seem to be blaming Thelma, even though she is just reading off script," Dianne said.

"No one should be blaming the weather announcer for the margin of error in probabilities widening. This is bound to happen because the weather is getting more unpredictable. People are also blaming the increase in violence on the weather and they are ignoring the increase in polarization between people," Jackson said.

"Tell me about it. Thelma emailed me yesterday that she was afraid to leave her office at the PPZ, alone. She said that her hate mail ranges from people blaming her for their lack of preparation for such bad weather, which makes them too hot, or too cold, too tired or too agitated, and sometimes just uncomfortably wet," Dianne said.

"And then we wonder why so many people are willing to give up their choices whenever the G.O.D. bot bureaucracies promise change and certainty. We just assume these bureaucratic changes will reduce all risk from our lives, by controlling everything and everyone, based on traits or what have you, but sooner or later we find out how these changes encroach on our freedoms," Jackson said.

"Family is everything, both of my parents always said that, even though we fought all the time we always loved each other a lot," Dianne replied.

"My family fought a lot too but I always felt like I belonged. If it weren't for all the love my parents gave us, we too could have been left in cages until we were age of majority. You know how those children live, under the care of the G.O.D. bots. They are brought up without much interaction or being allowed to integrate or belong. They are watched all the time, defined by buzzword sentences until every ounce of their creativity has been destroyed.

"That would be generous. Usually those kids are defined by one or two words," Dianne replied.

"And when they grow up they will be purged by the G.O.D. bots, one way or another," Jackson said.

"Without family a person is nothing these days," Dianne replied.

"Thank God for our parents. I still wish we had invited our parents to the wedding," Jackson said.

"Jackson, you know we didn't have time. And you know what my mother is like. At least Mary and David are sound asleep. Maybe time does heal everything even when the Exclusion League's G.O.D. bots are taking over nature and creation with its destruction and bad vibes. We have our parents to thank for not getting brainwashed into accepting destruction as the new normal," Dianne said.

As Jackson agreed with Dianne he glanced at his monitor and was thankful that the children were sound asleep, oblivious to this New World Order that would be dominating TV screens, everywhere, probably for the rest of their lives.

"News is not news anymore without someone getting personally attacked just for their appearance, especially for women, and too often lately, violently," Dianne said.

"I know, Di. But you have nothing to worry about. Your fans love you and always will," Jackson replied.

"This new kind of tension between people is different than I have ever experienced before. It like an abstract form of civil conflict is being fed through media so people's second nature begins to resent the economically disenfranchised and socially helpless, without even knowing why," Dianne said.

"I feel it too Di. This feeling of emptiness just grows on you, as if there was little power inside of one's psyche to fight it. It is like a feeling of being walled in," Jackson said.

"We are being walled in. Travel bans for the Minese, walls and tariffs. We are being cut off from the rest of the world. Imagine the power of this propagated hate could do to the mass psyche, especially when there are big groups of protesters or what have you? Such power either hardens you or makes you feel totally helpless and agitated. Imagine if the collective stream of consciousness grows even more impenetrable and less human while allowing the G.O.D. bots to cage little children as casually as they would cage a stray dog. And at the end of it all, martial law gives power to fools like Jethro and Bill and only family and good friends will be able to keep us sane," Jackson said.

"You can say that again," Dianne said as she hugged Jackson and gave him a lingering kiss.

Chapter 3: Sizing Things Up

March 17th 2031, around 4:30 PM

"If it is not one thing it is another," Maria said to Jennifer as she let Mathew's best friend walk in front of her. "And now we have these constant hurricane winds that never seem to end."

"I really thought those men on those military ships were going to shoot us with those evil looking projectiles. All those missiles being launched regardless of wind conditions or who is nearby," Jennifer replied.

"I was thinking the same thing," Maria said.

"Those men with their weapons drawn, aiming for the skies is a terrible reminder of what must have happened to Mathew. Those men really scare me even more than this weather does," Jennifer said.

"Statistically you have a far greater chance of getting hit by a stray projectile than lightning," Maria replied.

"I can believe it, and it all scares me," Jennifer said.

"When all those trees came crashing down on top of all those cars and trucks and homes, my heart felt like it was going to jump out of my chest. It all happened so quickly," Maria said.

"We seem to really be going backwards as a society. Sometimes I wonder if President Peel wants to send us back to the pre-industrial age, when there were so many wars going on, and when Tut territory had no allies," Jennifer said.

"Sometimes, I think President Peel is pulling us back beyond the Age of Enlightenment, the culture which pulled our ancestors forward from the tyranny of ignorance and authoritarianism," Maria said.

"And it seems that President Peel is leading us into an age of darkness which will pull us backward into a world with no allies," Jennifer said.

"The Age of Enlightenment was not just about one person. The Age of Enlightenment was about seeing light, where there was darkness and it was about listening in times of silence and trusting in a time of conflict and war. There was a birth of a higher self, of higher thinking, a higher consciousness. This new age of reason was not just about the rights of man, but understanding the power of being human. Many people who wanted more out of life, not just for themselves, but for others too, especially for those numbed by the despair of poverty, found ways to bring about positive change. They sought beauty that was found in art, literature, architecture, science, music, and hope; and spread it wherever they could," Maria said.

"In this age of war, paranoia and spying, we aren't making any new discoveries of our own that elevates us as a people, besides flyking of course. Our newest technologies keep us glued to our screens while scattering tracking sensors all over the place, watching us wherever we go. I have no idea how we could lose track of Mathew, there is some form of technology being used to keep us under surveillance everywhere. I never feel free on the ground the way I do when I flyke. When I flyke I feel free from being watched. I know the power of the mind is supposed to shape our future and who we will become, but all I feel is this dark regression surrounding me. Even though I keep wishing for progress to move my life forward, there is always one thing after another that keeps pulling me backwards," Jennifer said.

"I know what you mean. I keep hoping for something good to happen, instead another disaster happens." Maria said.

"I was really shocked when all those trees were being broken like matchsticks. I was so worried about getting hit by one of those flying missiles I forgot how dangerous a forest of trees could be, if they all were broken at once," Jennifer said as she clinged to her etherplayer.

"I don't know what scares me the most, the missiles whizzing by or this lightning storm. The electromagnetic activity being generated from all those black clouds never seems to stop. It follows you wherever you go. The light generating from the clouds is incredibly beautiful, but it seems really unnatural, to me. It is like an accumulation of energy stuck in those clouds, energy that will never die," Maria said."

"I was thinking the same thing, you just said it better," Jennifer said.

"Is your etherplayer okay? Maria asked as she placed her hands in the right position above the instrument until it wailed its usual eerie sound. "Mine seems fine."

Jennifer did the same.

"Yes, my etherplayer seems fine too. Don't you love the ghostly sounding vibes? It fits so well with a day like today," Jennifer said.

"The music sounds as ghostly as this violent windy weather does," Maria said.

"I really wish I knew where Mathew is," Maria said.

"If Mathew is alive he must be terrified. The search party found a bit of blood and a few of his flyke feathers so I think there is a good chance that he is still alive and holding on to his ground somewhere," Jennifer said.

"Every time I get an email from the search and rescue crew I am afraid that it is going to say they found pieces of Mathew here, and there and everywhere. And I was so thankful that all they found was a bit of blood and a few feathers. That means there is a good chance that he is still alive," Maria said.

"I sometimes wonder if I can actually feel his energy channeling near me. I know they may have killed Mathew's body and maybe Mathew's body is buried somewhere, but they can't kill his energy. I just know they can't. Maria are you going to get the door or should I?"

"I am getting the door," Maria said as she opened the door to Dianne's hotel suite.

"Hello James, I am surprised to see you here," Maria said.

"Hello, Maria. I am even more surprised to see you here, I am sure. Where are Dianne and Jackson? Where are the children? I thought they would all be home looking after each other until this terrible storm dies down. I was dropping off a gift basket and some toys for the little ones," James explained.

"Dianne and Jackson are out documenting this current weather disaster and they left the children downstairs in the hotel's maid quarters. One of the maid's daughters agreed to babysit for them. I was told that sometimes the maid's quarters can turn into a little mini daycare center if there are enough children dropped off there. The maids with young children drop their children off and the maids with older children take turns babysitting for them. The older children make a bit of money and the kids get a chance to play together and enjoy some of the diversions the hotel provides, like supervised splashing around in the swimming pool. The children seem to enjoy the swimming pool a lot and it gives everyone a break from all these disasters going on outside that never seem to end," Jennifer said.

"That is a great idea. Those kids will need to know how to swim with all these rainstorms and floods being forecasted for the future. I didn't know that the maids were so organized," James said, sounding a little concerned.

"I thought you knew everything that goes on in your

hotel, Mr. Coaltonstone. Dianne told me that you son, Alex has been funding some of these programs with your family foundation money," Jennifer said.

"Well, obviously I don't know everything," James said.

"I didn't know either until Dianne told me," Jennifer said.

"Obviously Dianne knows more than I do. What else did she tell you?"

"The musicians that play in the hotel bar are pretty organized too. Sometimes they leave their old musical instruments for the children to play with. Sometimes they show the children how to play them, and they also teach the children to sing in tune together. I thought I might take my etherplayer down their later, and show the children how it works," Jennifer said.

"I am sure the children would be thrilled. Sounds like a wonderful diversion from the current messy disaster going on outside," James said.

"Dianne invited me to stay here for a while, James, and I invited Jennifer," Maria explained "Dianne needs help with the children and I need help keeping my mind busy or I will drive myself crazy with worry about Mathew," Maria added.

"And this must be Jennifer" James said.

"Yes, James, I would like to introduce you to Jennifer Jones," Maria said.

"Pleased to meet you, Mr. Coaltonstone," Jennifer said.

"Jennifer is one of Mathew's closest friends. They have known each other since they were toddlers," Maria said as she gave James a quick hug.

"Isn't all this devastation heart wrenching. It is one devastating disaster after another. Part of Cold Feet Mountain falls on Coalton Two and now just when we think we are safe, all those trees come tumbling down on top of all those homes and cars that had managed to survive the terrible rock slide, and who knows what will happen next," James said.

"James, how can I feel heart wrenching pain over mere

things, when I am numb with grief over losing Mathew?" Maria asked as Jennifer bent over to give Maria a reassuring hug.

"Sometimes I think we would be better off without feelings. Without feelings, there would be no feelings to get hurt," James said.

"Mr. Coaltonstone, you don't really mean that do you?" Jennifer asked.

"I certainly do. Feelings just get in the way. When feelings get hurt, people don't apologize, they just hurt you more by causing trouble for you, especially these days," James said.

"But Mr. Coaltonstone, our feelings are what makes us human," Jennifer said.

"No Jennifer. Our feelings can be used against us, especially by those we love. Animals have feelings, we humans have thoughts," James said.

"But without love, what would motivate us to be considerate and care for each other?" Jennifer asked.

"Money and the force of the law," James said.

"James, really. We all know that greed motivates people to do all kinds of things to win big with no concern for those who lose everything. It feels like we are returning to the old times when feudalism and feuding were considered normal, and even noble" Maria said.

"I sort of believe that if you want loyal friends for life, get dogs," Jennifer said.

"Now, you are sounding like Mathew, he always wanted a dog. He kept saying my bot IQ was fun to hang out with, but a dog would be alive," James said.

"James, I think I am about to cry," Maria said.

"It is okay, Mrs. Watson. Things will be okay, I just know they will," Jennifer said.

"So, Mr. Coaltonstone, do you really think that the Minese government is weaponizing the weather with this new ice nucleation technology? What are your thoughts about that, Sir? Do you think global warming is causing rapid accumulation of bacteria? Do you think all these undocumented symptoms may be causing these scary storms?"

"Jennifer, you and Maria must be best of friends which is wonderful. I have enough on my plate worrying about undocumented aliens to worry about undocumented cloud and rainmakers. I don't have the time or inclination to worry about undocumented bacteria, either. If such stuff is causing extreme ice nucleation, there is not much that I can do about it except dress for the weather," James said.

"Jennifer, Mr. Coaltonstone doesn't believe in global warming," Maria explained.

"You don't, Sir? Is that because you are old?" Jennifer asked.

"Certainly not, I have not seen enough data to convince myself yet, Jennifer. I am an evidence based type of guy," James said, as he gave Jennifer a wink.

"Then how can you explain all these recent tornadic super cell storms? Jennifer asked.

"I can't, but I am not the only one who can't, Jennifer. That weather girl, on the PPZ is always getting the weather mixed up," James said defensively.

"Do you think the Minese government is using this new weather technology against us, or do you think we are using this new technology against them and it is backfiring on us?" Jennifer asked.

"All I know is that the Minese government is accusing our side of causing these terrible tornadic super cell storms and they seem to be here, but some of these storms might be happening over there, too. We get a lot of news blackouts these days, so who knows what is going on. My guess is either side, if they felt that they were in control of this cloud seeding technology would try to weaponize it, especially now with President Peel in charge, anything could happen. Probably the only thing stopping a sane person from using this technology is the fear that the technology could backfire somehow. But then I have my doubts about President Peel's sanity," James said.

"I agree, it is frightening that a fool on either side could be weaponizing the cloud seeding technology and is manipulating the weather like this," Maria said.

"Such idiots would never admit it either," James said.

"Imagine fools using airborne silver iodide generators to torment their adversaries," Maria said.

"I remember the simple days when predicting the weather was a hit and miss science, but we were able to blame Mother Nature for the outcome. Now we have no idea who to blame. The only thing that hasn't changed is we still can't predict the weather effectively enough to divert the storm clouds and maybe use all this rain for good, like putting out wild fires in the summer time," James said.

"I know we still don't know a lot about the dangers of airborne silver iodide generators and the impact they could have on cloud-to-ground lightning, but common sense doesn't prevail much any more. As far as I can see, regardless if this weather phenomenon is being generated by bacteria due to global warming, or it is being induced by weaponized weather technology, this situation could be imposing an unnatural threat to mankind, on a global level," Maria warned.

"You mean peoplekind, right Maria?" James interjected.

"Of course," Maria replied.

"All this new weather technology and politics is way too complicated for me. I am just a simple miner," James said.

"James," Maria laughed.

"Aren't you kind of old to be a miner?" Jennifer asked.

"Jennifer!" Maria scolded.

"Young lady, must I remind you that life is too short to let it define you," James said.

"Mr. Coaltonstone, what do you mean by that?" Jennifer asked.

"I, young lady am a self-made man. It is not what I am, it is who I am. I am James Coaltonstone. My physical characteristics may be beyond my control, but I am still steering the wheel of fate," James said.

"I didn't know you believed in the wheel of fate, James," Maria said.

"I would be a fool to not keep my hands on the steering wheel so that it didn't start to spin out of control," James said as he winked at Jennifer again. "Of course my physical characteristics matter, my body contains my life. Regardless of my physical attributes, which are pretty incredible may I add."

"For a man your age, they sure are," Jennifer interjected.

"Jennifer!" Maria scolded, again.

"I have the fitness level of a man half my age, and twice the intelligence."

"Everyone thinks they are smarter than everyone else because they are satisfying the primal needs of their reptilian ego," Jennifer said.

"Jennifer Jones," Maria interjected.

"Your point, child?" James asked.

"Who we are, is what we bring to the next level," Jennifer said.

"Are you any relation to Susan Jones, by any chance?" James asked as he held on to Jennifer's hand, giving Jennifer good reason to feel startled.

"Yes, I am her cousin, twice removed, or something like that," Jennifer explained.

"Why am I not surprised?" James wondered out loud. "Oh, I suppose being twice removed, as cousins, explains why you look so different than her," James said as he reluctantly released Jennifer's hand.

"Can we get back to why we are here? We are looking for my grandson, which Jennifer and I believe is still alive and is in trouble and needs our help," Maria said.

"Maria, I hope he is alive too, but there is a greater chance that he isn't," James replied.

"If Mathew is alive, and we do nothing, he will die due to our negligence and our self fulfilling prophesying," Maria said.

"Mathew is in this situation because of Jethro and Bill, not you Maria," Jennifer said softly.

"Yes, but I was the one who gave him his flyke-suit, and encouraged him to flyke and enjoy the beauty of the heavens and all the nature directly below," Maria said as a tear dropped from her eye. "He loved flyking with the birds. He seemed to have been developing a sixth sense, like some kind of internal compass. He never seemed to get lost. He always seemed to know where he was going and how to get back. Doctor Knight used to say he probably has some form of magnetite based receptors in his brain the way birds have on their beaks," Maria said. "There is also a possibility that Mathew was exposed to blue light, enough light to develop magnetorecption through the cryptochrome protein in his eyes."

"That is really going beyond probabilities Maria, don't you think?" James said.

"Not necessarily, there is not a lot known about the pairing phenomenon, human between the life forces which surround us, or even about the process of magnetorecption. We do know that process works for migratory birds, so why not for migratory humans? It may be that our alienation from Mother Nature and our own nature has led to the loss of our homing instinct. I believe we still have the chemistry to revive our sixth sense and to feel more at home in our natural surroundings," Maria said.

"This is all very fascinating but what does this have to do with finding Mathew?" James asked.

"Because there are forces in this universe that are far greater than ourselves. We hope those forces will protect Mathew. Some people believe that it doesn't matter if we understand these great and powerful forces. All we need to do is try to communicate to them, in prayer or meditation. The electromagnetic field has two forces, positive and a negative charge. While gravity is the curvature of space-time, so if Mathew fell, when he was shot, he wouldn't have just fallen in a straight line. So wherever Mathew landed depends on how much space-time there was between the places where he was shot and where he landed. The process goes on regardless of how little we understand it or even care about it," Maria said.

"It is hard not to care, the beauty is captivating. Keeping your eyes and mind open is part of the process too, Mr. Coaltonstone, to soak in the world's beauty, before it is all lost. Willing to see the blue light, and to feel the power of positivity pulling us up when all the negativity in this world is pulling us down, is everything beyond point zero. It is where we turn everything around and make it great again," Jennifer said

"Easy for a youngster to say that, blue light can also strain if not damage your eyes. You will find that out soon enough, as you get older. Besides everything in life is about balance. Too much of a good thing can do damage. A little of a good thing could create a spark for a new invention," James said.

"You are lecturing us about moderation, James," Maria mocked back.

"How can you be receptive without receptors? Really Maria," James said.

"By opening your eyes and your mind a bit, Mr. Coaltonstone," Jennifer said.

"We don't need another barrier that blocks us from our subconscious abilities. People get trapped in opposite poles when they argue, because we are socially engineered that way. If you are looking at Earth's rotation above the North Pole, it is turning counter-clockwise. But then if you look at Earth's rotation above the South Pole, it is rotating clockwise. That is really something. Super confusing but really something. This is the way people are conditioned to be so polarized, as far as I can see," Jennifer said.

"How do you know so much about Earth's spinning rotation?" James asked.

"We are studying it at school, Mr. Coaltonstone. The earth is always rotating. Always spinning, just like time," Jennifer said. "Mass creates a gravitational field so we are pushed into it by the force of space-time, and where we land, is where our path starts, continues or ends. People argue that gravity is or isn't a force..." Jennifer said before James interrupted her.

"And who wins the argument?" James asked.

"In theory the right answer is supposed to be evidence based. In practice it is all about who gets the funding, and whether the findings could be weaponized in the future, as far as I can see. It is sort of like trying to monetize the value of optimism, confidence and being positive. A person who believes that something can work can often make something work. If they don't believe something will work, how can they make it work? The life force gives us existence and then we can verify that the life force exists, but it would exist anyway, with or without us. We live because we are protected by gravity's force field. Our journey in time-space is lengthened just because we don't land up floating into our atmosphere and burning up. Energy never dies, it transforms but never dies. It is all really incredibly beautiful, don't you think, Mr. Coaltonstone?"

"It all sounds like a mind game to me. If Earth stood still, would time? Doesn't time age us? Look at me. Look how many rotations Earth has made, since I have been on it?" James said.

"No Sir, it is the gravitational field which, in theory, warps space-time. And time affects the chemicals, which decay and age us. Super massive gravity fields slow down time, you know the type found in black holes," Jennifer said.

"Sometimes I wish the world would stop spinning, or start spinning backwards in time, so I could de-age," James said. "I hate getting old."

"Why would anyone want to see Earth stop spinning? Without Earth's slightly tilted spinning, we would have no variety in seasons. If the earth stopped spinning, our day and night would not be as we know them to be. Without Earth spinning, a day would be around 365 'our days'. Without Earth's rotation we would have no rest from the scorching sun and the motion of the oceans would turn to chaos. The way the earth rotates, day to night and season to season, is one of the most incredible things about life on Earth, how energy just lives in endless eternity, includes our own time frame, our own existence," Jennifer said.

"And we take all these unexplained forces for granted," Maria said.

"Why does a girl like you, Jennifer, worry about energy living in eternity and such things?" James asked. "You are young. Time is on your side, why worry about it at all?"

"Ever since Mathew was shot down, I wonder where or what he might be, now. I know I will be wondering, for the rest of my life, what happened to him. I wonder a lot more about the secrets of the universe now too. I wonder about life, death and stuff beyond what we know as mere mortals. And other times, all I can think about is wishing that Mathew could be by my side, again. Never knowing what happened to Mathew will haunt me for the rest of my life. If the great unexplained can turn around the Earth, why can't they turn around what happened to Mathew?" Jennifer said.

"I understand where you are coming from Jennifer, but you must continue with your life and work around the black hole in your life that Mathew left behind or it will suck away your very existence, and you will lose out on your future. You know Mathew would want you to find a way to turn it all around. But thinking about deep things like eternity will just drive you crazy," James said.

"You don't think about eternity, Mr. Coaltonstone? If I were as old as you are, I would be thinking about it all the time," Jennifer said.

"Never had the time to worry about such things. I have always been too busy making money, taking care of things and my work. Going out and looking for new sources of coal. Who has time to ponder the secrets of the universe when all we can do is speculate anyway? We interpret things the way we need to, and so far I don't need to be thinking about eternity, I spend my time thinking about making money," James said.

"That is why we probably take life for granted, until someone you love is taken away from you. Once you lose someone you love, a huge black hole inside you starts to grow. The emptiness makes you wonder if it is all worth it. You begin to doubt if you are strong enough to cope. You start to think about immortality and all that stuff and the fragile balance which holds life and sanity all together," Jennifer said.

"We just don't have the time to be thinking about all those things," James said.

"Our own time of existence in relation to eternity is just like a speck of sand, Jennifer," Maria said.

"If President Peel has his way, we will all be moving backwards in time. Using financial models that are over two hundred years old could send us back to those dark times," James said.

"Yeah, we never take the time to think about the eternal power of time, and stuff. Sort of ironic, don't you think, Mr. Coaltonstone, considering how long we are dead for, you think we would be taking time to think about how precious life really is," Jennifer said.

"My theory is when you go beyond this physical world, you also go beyond self and the state of time. And without all that, you become aware of some form of Eternity, that is already here, but we never take the time to think about the next level, which of course must be endless," Maria interjected.

"How do you know if Eternity exists at all?" James asked.

"I don't know, but it makes sense that Eternity goes on because energy never dies. I am not the only who believes that Eternity is not just on the other side but it is the extension of what is, on our side. A lot of people believe in Eternity, James," Maria said.

"I certainly can understand why," James said.

"Regardless if we are being pulled or pushed, these forces are protecting us every micro-second of our lives, from floating up into our atmosphere and burning out of existence, as if who we are in our present form, never mattered at all," Jennifer said.

"What I find just as fascinating is the chance that we have the biology which could develop into a sixth sense. It is said, due to our ancient ancestry, we might actually have the chemistry in our eyes to home in on our destinies. So little is known about the power of our sixth sense, the power of our ancient selves. We know more about coal than our ancient links to Earth, and that is a tragedy," Maria said.

"Speak for yourself, Maria. When I was just fifteen years old, around Mathew's age, I thought coal was everything. I thought about cars, and girls and of course, but I knew, even at such a young age, the world turns around coal," James said.

"The only boy I ever thought about was Mathew, Mr. Coaltonstone," Jennifer said as she barely was able to stop herself from crying.

"Mathew is lost, not because of lack of ability, but lack of luck. If Mathew is alive he needs our help. If he is dead then we need our own help. We should dedicate our lives, if necessary in the search for Mathew. When we find him, we have gained closure. We should also find the right spot to lay Mathew to rest. If necessary, so that he can rest in peace for the rest of eternity," James said.

"Sometimes I wonder if the forces in the sky are the greatest cloud seeders of all," Maria said.

"I wonder that all the time," Jennifer said.

"Sometimes I wonder if all these hurricanes are just reflecting the anger, we humans are conditioned to feel for others who are different and have the nerve to compete for the rare resources that we either need or want," Maria said.

"Sometimes I wonder how much of this global warming and rapid growth of bacteria is responsible for the growth of all those ice-nucleation proteins, which could lead to a supernatural cloud seeding process that could only get worse. Maybe drown millions," Jennifer said.

"I always wondered the same thing about all the smog coal causes," Maria said.

"Coal has been generating the steam and electricity to run many of the engines of the world for over two hundred years. There are records that prove that coal was used long before 3,000 BC, especially in Mina. Coal mining has given work to idle people, warmth to cold people, and a substance to generate fire for hungry people to cook on. The coal market gives all of us a chance to meet our neighbors and help each other out with our human development. Coal has probably helped to keep peoplekind alive, big time," James said

"Are you saying without coal we would not have civilisation as we know it?" Jennifer asked

"I certainly am. Coal is one of Earth's most important gifts to peoplekind," James said.

"It can also cause bad karma," Maria said. "There must be lot of truth surrounding the Black Diamond Curse or the tale wouldn't have been passed from generation to generation the way it has."

"Are you saying that coal poses a lot more than a moral hazard, the karma connected to coal acts like a curse?" Jennifer asked.

"What isn't a moral hazard or karma induced? We humans are physically weaker than most of the other species that are living on our planet, and in many ways we are alienated from Earth and each other, big time. We develop our lives, often by staying and working indoors, by fireplaces and coal pits. We cook our food, we make metals to provide us with transportation, because we humans have to make our own wheels and wings. Of course coal doesn't tumble out of the sky, we have to dig deep into the ground to discover it, and then mine it. The coal channels the energy needed to keep economies moving, especially in less developed parts of the world," James said.

"And coal makes it almost impossible for frail people to breathe the air and stay healthy at the same time," Jennifer said.

"Jennifer why are you always arguing with me? All through history nature is culling its flock," James said. "Coal creates steam to channel energy and economic progress."

"Talking about steam that is one thing I am running out of. I am trying to channel all my energy to find my grandson. James, how could you manage to indirectly kill my two Mathews during my lifetime? Parents are not supposed to outlive their children and no one expects to outlive their grandchildren," Maria said.

"That is not fair Maria. I did not kill your two Mathews. They were both victims of an unfortunate set of circumstances way beyond all of our control. Just like this terrible storm that is destroying property and putting lives at risk. These are the End Times that we were warned about, by the Good Book. So anyone know what are they calling this current tornadic super cell thunderstorm?" James asked.

"They are calling it Popeye Two, I believe. Strange name for a thunderstorm," Maria said.

Chapter 4

Jackson and Dianne Find Mathew's Camera

March 17th 2031, around 5:00 PM: "Dianne, are you sure you want to search the site. Maybe we should let the G.O.D. bots take the lead," Jackson suggested as Dianne stepped carefully over the debris.

"No, we need to take the lead before the G.O.D. bots decree into law that we can't search for unidentified flying objects, which technically Mathew could be considered," Dianne said. "Keep your light on but don't run the camera. I have this feeling if Mathew is alive or even if he isn't, if he could he would have tried to leave us a message or something. You know Mathew and his pictures, they all had some unwritten story in each frame. If Mathew is alive we need to find him."

"Big if," Jackson said.

"What in life isn't 'a big if', especially these days?" Dianne retorted.

"Di, the yellow tape is surrounding this site for a reason you would think something would be guarding it," Jackson said as he looked around.

"Chances are something is guarding it. We are PPZ journalists. We are supposed to be taking risks for the common good, regardless of red tape or yellow tape or any other color of tape," Dianne said.

"We are also a newlywed couple in the process of adopting David and Mary," Jackson said.

"Yes, and we still live in a world where freedom of the press is allowed. Jackson, I see something," Dianne said. "Down there. I will hold your camera, go down there and look."

After Jackson worked himself down the hill, he bent over and picked up a camera.

"It looks like Mathew's camera, I would recognize it anywhere. He always had MW stickers all over his camera. The glass is broken but it seems to be working. He seems to have taken a lot of pictures," Jackson said.

"That was Mathew for you. He always felt the most alive when he was flyking in the heavens and taking photographs of the happenings below," Maria said.

"I really feel that Mathew is alive," Jennifer said.

"I agree," Maria said.

"What are you two ladies doing here?" Dianne asked, knowing that they must have followed her to the site. "Who is looking after the children?"

"We followed you," Maria explained. "The maid's daughter said she would baby-sit for us. She is expecting a child of her own, and needs practice, according to her mother."

"Hey Di, look at Mathews frames, they are really something," Jackson said as he rushed up the hill.

"Those pictures are really are so candid, so alive," Maria said. "Mathew really loved taking photos that reflected real life. He admired you so much, Jackson. He often said he would like to be a great cameraman and maybe work for PPZ like you do and stand beside a beautiful war correspondent, like Dianne. Jennifer has often said that she would like to be just like you, Dianne. Mathew often thought about the work he might do in a distant war torn places across the ocean, and so does Jennifer, don't you dear?"

"Yes, Mrs. Watson I sometimes do. Other times I fancy myself and Mathew working for National Geographic, or another famous publication like that," Maria said.

"I bet it never crossed Mathew's mind that he would be shot down in Tut territory by friendly fire. Mathew was always thrilled after he sold his photos to you. And Jennifer was always so proud of Mathew, weren't you Jennifer?" Maria asked.

"Yes, Mathew was such a great photographer. He wanted to show the entire world how beautiful it is, and he was so generous. He always gave half of his earnings to 'Save the Whales and all Sea Creatures Society," Jennifer said.

"I didn't know that," Maria said.

"Yes, that charity had the highest ratings, on the charity navigator. We picked the charity together," Jennifer said.

"That is so sweet," Dianne said.

"Mathew believed that the whales were smarter than the average human and that they understood the workings of our Earth, better than we did. It was amazing how he took such great pictures while flyking," Jennifer said.

"You both helped Mathew feel that his pictures had value and were worth something," Maria said.

"Mathew had a great eye," Jackson said.

"Mathew has a great eye. I just know that he is still alive. That picture is a message, obviously," Jennifer said. "And no photograph would ever be worth a person's life. It is stupid to risk your life just to take a photograph," Jennifer said.

"Mathew had a great love for the world around him, and there was no one I ever met that understood how endangered beauty always is. Beauty is temporary, just like life," Jackson said.

"But energy never dies," Jennifer said

"It looks like a picture of two scarecrows tied to poles," Dianne said.

Jackson zoomed in.

"Now look," Jackson said.

"Oh my God," Dianne said.

CHAPTER 5:

Are G.O.D. Bots In Control Of Weather, Now?

March 17th 2031, around 5:30 PM: "So what side of the Great Wall do you like best, Mr. Coaltonstone? The Minese side or our side?" Jennifer asked.

"Are you talking about that ugly new wall I almost drove into on the way here?" James asked.

"I can't believe that President Peel and his Exclusion League imposed this horrible thing upon us. It changes the direction of the traffic flow, big time. I feel so bad for the businesses that were thriving when we had open access to both sides of the border," James said.

"As if life on Tut Island wasn't hard enough, since President Peel and the Exclusion League take over life has been plagued with uncertainty," Maria said.

"Why am I even investing the last few years I might still have on this earth, and billions of dollars in such hostile market conditions? I am participating in a joint project that will change the world and move the global economy forward, while President Peel and his Exclusion League are walling us all in and pulling us back into a time when the Tut territory was isolated and had no allies. President Peel's politics is all about social engineering to gain political advantage over everyone who is not part of his inner circle. Walling us only causes chaos and confusion. So why am I trying to change the world?" James asked nobody in particular, and wasn't even expecting an answer.

"Mr. Coaltonstone, if you can change the world, you should. I sure would if I could," Jennifer said.

"I and my colleagues are about to complete the Bering Strait Hyper-Loop Rail Peace Complex between Eurasia and North America. This project is a peace offering and could be a step in the right direction to end world hunger, by stimulating new markets and quicken the pace of world travel and shipping," "James said.

"Is President Peel going to allow you to complete such a project?" Jennifer asked.

"I refuse to be walled in by President Peel or anyone else. My hyper-loop rail service will be connecting North America with Eurasia. It is my dream and I am going to live it. President Peel and his Exclusion League be dammed," James said.

"Are you sure that President Peel isn't going to make trouble for you? I mean he just put up a wall surrounding Tut territory, which means that connecting Mina with North America is not big on his agenda," Jennifer said.

"How dare President Peel assume he has the power to wall me in? I am James Coaltonstone, I am subservient to no one," James said.

"Maybe you need a code name for your hyper-loop rail service. The name is rather long anyway," Maria said.

"My project does have a code name, we call it the Pea, sort of the way the Volkswagen was called the Bug," James said.

"What are you talking about, I have never heard of anything called a Bug," Jennifer said.

"Kids from Jennifer's generation aren't familiar with those antique cars, James," Maria said.

"President Peel won't stop me or wall me in, that will be my legacy, to never be walled in. Sooner or later, my legacy will outlive his legacy, because mine will be bigger and more beautiful. This dream of mine to connect Eurasia with North America will not die by getting walled in, I refuse to let that happen," James said.

"The Exclusion League backers might say that you are aiding and embedding the enemy by defying the wall which is protecting us from outsiders," Maria replied.

"That word embedding, it sounds like you are in bed with outsiders," Jennifer said.

"Jennifer, really," Maria scolded.

"I am really being besieged and stifled by insiders.. I will not have my global vision walled in by a megalomaniac," James said.

"Good for you, James," Maria said.

"I will not have my scope of vision narrowed and my future finalised by a demagogue that believes that he and his insiders have a right to dominate the planet, and to leave all outsiders out of the economy. This policy will only assassinate my markets not protect them. This has nothing to do with sleeping with the enemy. No one is sleeping and we are at technically at war with the Minese government not the Minese people," James said.

"At times I think that President Peel is at war with us," Jennifer said.

"Technically we are outsiders too, but in a different way. Every new policy which is being made my President Peel, favors the insiders," James said.

"President Peel is making young people outsiders too. I know kids who are terrified that their numbers are going to be the ones drawn in the draft lottery. It is the uncertainty, which drives people crazy. Not knowing what is going to happen next but realizing that only President Peel and his inner circle have a political interest in lowering the number of people available to work. Keep us out of employment gives the people of voting age a higher chance of finding jobs. So whatever is politically advantageous for President Peel, he will do, regardless of who is left out in the cold. Sometimes I wonder if President Peel started this war with the Minese government so he could have an excuse to draft kids between the ages of eighteen and twenty-five and have a war zone to send them to," Jennifer said.

"Of course he did. What every President Peel does is about politics.. I won't let my dream die or let my markets be assassinated by travel bans, tariffs, war-walls and wall-wars," James said. "And Jennifer don't let your dreams die, either, let them grow and live the best way you know in your heart is right for you."

"My dream was to spend my life with Mathew and to be a team, the way Dianne Black and Jackson Green are," Jennifer said.

"Dreams change, but once you are on a path, you may find no way off. I am focusing on my dream project because I know how it is going to expand markets and create new pockets of wealth, not just for Peel's insiders but for all kinds of people. For years, we have been boring multipurpose tunnels, using funds, my own and associates, to manufacture the capsules, tubes, and freight cars to make my hyper-loop rail service a reality," James said.

"James, you really are moving forward, in these terrible times," Maria said.

"All that President Peel and his Exclusion League backers can think of doing is to wall us all in while picking fights with people who have less socio-economic power than the average person does. I hate it when insiders look down at outsiders and sabotage their chance for success. It is not just sick and selfish, it increases market risk for everyone but them. Walling in outsiders gives the insiders a chance to look down at us while treating us all like bums," James said.

"It is really hypocritical isn't it? Immigrants are brought in, not so they can have a better life, so business and society can build railways, farm and mine far cheaper than if they had to pay the citizen-workers a liveable wage. The more undocumented the immigrants are, the more vulnerable they are too exploitation and abuse. Instead of building a better life, here, they will find themselves trapped in perpetual servitude to others who gain the most when these people are exploited the most," Maria said.

"Being forced to where an 'M' on their left breast will only make their conditions worse," Jennifer said.

"You think?" James said.

"You can see their vulnerability wherever you go. They are even smaller than we are," Jennifer said.

"Immigrants are self-segregating most of the time, for good reason. We could make their life easier, instead that demagogue Peel exploits our prejudices, and he wins the election. The most ignorant enjoy making life for the Minese as difficult as possible. It gives them a feeling of power, which they usually don't have. I think that is what President Peel exploits," Maria said.

"All those unwritten rules to keep immigrants apart from the mainstream, give those people a chance to boss the immigrants and vagrants around, and for a moment they feel powerful and feel a sense of pride in that. And the time that they are wasting getting caught in that horrible spiral of bigotry," Jennifer said.

"Most of us are weakened by time, the later it gets in the day, the weaker we get, why waste it in being mean to people. We can always change our mind about people, but we can't change our deeds," Maria said.

"Now that tariffs and counter-tariffs are making materials much more expensive, we will need more undocumented workers than we ever did. And though most people say they don't want immigration, our entire society benefits by keeping supply of labor up and prices of consumer goods down," James said.

"You mean it is good for the owners, not necessarily for citizen-workers who are legally entitled to be paid minimum wage unless they have agreed to contract work," Maria said.

"I suppose, but I know for a fact that President Peel has used undocumented workers in his own enterprises, especially when dirty or dangerous work has to be done. Whenever he wanted to pay far less than minimum wage, he used undocumented workers to do that work," James said.

"The more undocumented the workers are, the more vulnerable they will be to all kinds of exploitation and abuse," Maria said.

"Sometimes I think that President Peel wouldn't care so much about immigration as an issue, if it didn't stir up so much resentment among unemployed citizen-workers. A lot of the unemployed feel if it weren't for the immigrants, the owners would have to pay a decent wage, or at least minimum wage," Jennifer said.

"And when President Peel is not stereotyping the most vulnerable people in our community on Twitter, he is attacking the world leaders on Twitter. Many of those world leaders used to be our allies, but President Peel's polices and Twitter attacks are walling us in from our allies and a world we used to know," James said.

"Why do you think President Peel, with all his money and power is so unhappy?" Jennifer asked.

"I think the president's wife is repulsed by him," James said.

"That makes sense," Jennifer said.

"It sure does," Maria agreed. "I am repulsed by him too."

"I think there are many kinds of ghettos, and the president lives in his," Jennifer said. "I think there should be a maximum wage, and not just a minimum wage. Why does someone need to be a billionaire or even a trillionaire, especially when there are so many homeless and starving people living on the streets, in camps and reservations? All that money doesn't make him happy. Look at him. All he does is yell at people and he has this constant turnover. Our republic is becoming authoritarian and doesn't show common courtesy to smaller and less wealthy nations."

"It would take a violent revolution I suppose to introduce a maximum wage," Maria said. "The super rich are always afraid of violence. They don't seem to consider targeting the most vulnerable for incarceration and 'Pay to Stay" initiatives, is the same type of violence that supported slavery. We are going back to that way of life, where social mobility is seen as anti-social. The rich get mega-rich, and sometimes so greedy it becomes a sickness, and the poor get so poor, they can't even sustain life, so they deteriorate rapidly."

"Sometimes President Peel even attacks Twitter, even though Twitter is a free service and gives millions if not billions of people a voice. A voice that would never be heard, otherwise," Jennifer said.

"President Peel seems to be mad at everyone and at everything, even though our republic was supposed to be governance for the people, by the people. And he acts outraged if anyone appears to be doing better than he is doing, and then up goes the walls and barriers and no-entry signs. Everything is sum-zero for him. That seems to be the primary model he uses for every situation that comes up especially when someone is gaining on socio-economic power, and may soon have more than he does. Then up go the barriers and walls, not to mention the way President Peel starts assassinating previous trade agreements. Talk about violence, he out-shouts everyone. And he never seems to pick those fights face to face. He picks fights over Twitter so his victims are cornered in, when getting picked on by technically the most powerful man in the universe," James said. "I build peace-connectors, he builds war-walls and he wins the election. The irony defies the imagination."

"I won't be intimidated by that man, I believe in the principles of our republic, governance for the people by the people," James said.

"Easier to say James, even the scientists are becoming wilfully blind, and no longer making current observations," Maria said.

"Everyone needs to be braver. This is home of the free and the brave isn't? Why have we become a country of slaves, near-slaves and the timid?" James asked.

"That wall looks hard, cold and evil, and it surrounds us," Maria replied.

"That wall looks like just another war-wall to me and it is surrounding our republic," Jennifer said.

"That is exactly what I am saying. The irony of it all; I am building a peace connector between North America and Eurasia to link us, which is great and beautiful, and he is building a wall to separate us from our world markets and countries who used to be our allies. My hyper-loop rail network will save a tremendous amount of travel and shipping time related costs, and will break barriers. President Peel is building a war-wall that will guzzle money and time, while holding back everyone who is trying to cross the border. President Peel is creating one barrier after another. There is nothing great about that horrible wall, with its barbed wire fencing and places for guards and botguards to stand and watch the people below as if they were mere ants. And then there is that platform where the drones land on, which is collecting all kinds of surveillance data on people nearby. People don't realize how many sensors they are actually carrying on their person, and how easy it is to track them. If only this administration would have worked with me on my Bering Strait Hyper-Loop Rail Peace Complex, it would have been completed much faster and we would have been expanding, not contracting our economy by now," James said.

"That wall looks nothing like a peace crossing or friendship crossing by any stretch," Jennifer said.

"That wall is totally out of place and is stupid, considering most of the Minese use the hidden and mostly undocumented tunnel system to get around. They have always stayed out of our way, and usually we stay out of their way. There are all kinds of tunnels, all over Tut Island. Some of these tunnels actually go all the way to Tut Metropolis and even to Mina territory. Soon there will be connector tunnels linking Eurasia and North America," James said.

"Mr. Coaltonstone, is it possible that Mathew landed on the wrong side of that wall?" Jennifer asked.

"I guess he could have, that explain why we are finding it hard to locate him. It is also possible that we are on the wrong side of the wall. Nothing is the same any more since President Peel was elected. Sometimes I feel like I am in a prison, in my own country. My markets are being assassinated by these tariffs, and people I have known for years in the security community, are having their security clearance revoked. Sometimes I wonder if Mathew would have been shot down if he had been flyking on the Minese side of the wall," James said.

"Anything is possible, these days," Maria said. "I mean that wall went up pretty quickly. If Mathew had some steam left to flyke, and didn't know that the wall was there, or what it was for, he could have landed on the wrong side of the wall. That would mean he is technically an illegal and a vagrant over there. If he is caught he could be sentenced to years of hard labor as a slave. He doesn't know Minese but many of the Minese know how to speak English. Would they speak English to him is another matter," Maria said.

"As we were discussing earlier, Mathew wouldn't be falling out of the sky in a straight line when he was shot, he would have had space-time curving his fall and possibly he had some steam left to create distance between himself and those idiots who shot him," James said.

"The more you think about it, the more it makes sense that Mathew could have fallen behind that war-wall. Another irony is it always depends on what side of the wall you are standing when defining which side is the good side and which side is the bad side. These wars are escalating hostilities between nations that the tariffs and counter-tariffs ignited. It is just ordinary people killing people just like themselves, while the rich grow richer and the poor grow so much poorer. Which side is President Peel really on? He must have known this was going to happen? You are right Mr. Coaltonstone, the sides are really blurry aren't they?" Jennifer asked.

"And most importantly this war is threatening the existence of our republic," James said.

"This is a big change in the conversation, I thought we were talking about Mathew," Maria said.

"Well, we are. And if Mathew is caught in a war zone, he could be treated like a spy and his fate could be worse than death," Jennifer said.

"So could ours, on this side of the wall, with a demagogue acting lie a self appointed judge, juror and executioner," James said.

"Jennifer and James, don't be so melodramatic," Maria interjected.

"I am not being melodramatic. I am just taking being at war seriously," Jennifer replied.

"And the fact that our republic was meant to be free of tyranny, also should be taken seriously. This is the land of the free and brave, and someone needs to stand up to President Peel," James said.

"Everyone is afraid of him because he can make life very unpleasant when he wants to," Maria replied.

"I know, and he seems to enjoy it, especially when the unpleasantness starts to grow legs and the Exclusion League backers take it to the next level. The culture here has changed so much, I don't recognize where I am anymore. The president acts like a cult leader, only accountable to himself. As long as President Peel has a lot of money and power, he has worshippers," James said.

"I understand, but when you two talk like that, be careful, someone might be listening. There are sensors everywhere. I have seen people leave after interrogations looking like Zombies. They must have been drugged with something very powerful, or were given electric shocks. I also heard that they are bringing back forced lobotomies," Maria said.

"If you want my opinion, Jennifer, I think wars are either just plain stupid or they are being deliberately designed to provoke people to justify killing them. And when a person sees such brutality, it changes them. Coal may be a dirty business, but the industry of war is dirtier and probably a lot more lucrative. We keep asking ourselves what side we are on, but we never ask what side President Peel is on. After the war, there are always fewer people left competing for resources, jobs and pensions. When this war is over, there will be far fewer people left to convince that the huge gap between the rich and the poor is for society's own good. The cult of personality could then be transformed into a money worshipping cult," James said.

"James, don't you think that it is you now, being melodramatic?" Maria asked.

"Maybe, but I might be right. If they start writing in 'God We Trust' on their currency, that would be a clue that I am right. Putting money above people would be another clue. The new law that condemns people to death if they have served fifteen or more years in prison, often for crimes of poverty, could be a third clue. Such a cult could serve to decrease the population too. Shooting people at demonstrations who are protesting unfair laws could also cull the population of mostly poor people," James said.

"Mr. Coaltonstone, I didn't know that you were so super revolutionary, I always thought that you were super draconian. Do you think this war is not really between countries but between the rich and poor?" Jennifer replied.

"Ever since Mathew was shot down I feel different about a lot of things, Jennifer," James said.

"I thought you were too old to change the way you saw the world, Mr. Coaltonstone," Jennifer said.

"I did too, Jennifer," James said.

"Do you think President Peel might change the way he sees to the world, too?" Jennifer asked.

I really doubt it. I am too old to wait around to find out. I am determined to get my hyper-loop rail service working, while I still can. I don't know if President Peel wants to change," James said.

"Maybe President Peel has spent too much time wheeling and dealing and never took the time to think about the power of goodwill," Jennifer said.

"I am not going to wait for President Peel to change his mind. My peace connector between North America and Eurasia is already behind schedule. I believe someone standing up and taking the initiative can create goodwill between opposing forces. Standing up to President Peel would take a lot more courage, than fighting to the death in his battles, and might also save our republic," James said.

"President Peel is all about President Peel, he doesn't even seem to understand that our republic was meant to prevent tyranny, and have government run for and by the people. He openly flaunts dehumanising vagrants on Twitter, encouraging his supporters to do the same. The president's experts talk about rehabilitation as if these people did some horrible crime, and he flatly denies that 'Pay to Stay and Stay to Pay' isn't about overcharging the destitute, to keep them out of sight and out of mind, while turning them into slaves," Maria said.

"Jobs just naturally integrate people. People go to work, mingle, meet other people, live in homes and can dress like decent people. When the Social Problem takes over, and jobs are lost, it is never seems to define the inability to integrate displaced people as a socio-economic problem. If anything

President Peel attacks these people, using his Twitter feed as bad people,

"He denies that the Social Problem, is a symptom of economical hardship, and as the richest get richer and the poorest get poorer, some of the poorest will be making life and death decisions when facing their own food insecurity issue," Jennifer said.

"The entire situation confuses me and I am trying to focus on my new hyper-loop rail service before one of my adversaries beats me to it," James said.

"I see leaders visiting other countries that we used to be enemies with, and they are setting up their own security fences while talking to people, through them. It seems like everyone is talking through walls of fear and mutual disdain, lately," Maria said.

"The world leaders are not even trying to build trust between each other. They are just putting out fires caused by tariffs and counter-tariffs, devaluation of local currencies and uncontrolled inflation and hyperinflation. No wonder alienation and a sadistic meanness, is taking over at the highest levels of government," James said.

"I often wonder the same thing, Mr. Coaltonstone," Jennifer said.

"These are very painful times that we are living in. I don't think this war is so much about good and evil as it is about being on the winning side and the losing side. And I am not sure if we are on the winning side. Hopefully we win this war and we are able find Mathew in one piece," James said.

"I know exactly what you are saying Mr. Coaltonstone. It is really hard to know what side Jethro and Bill are on too. Mathew was shot down by people on our side while he was flyking on our side of the wall," Jennifer said.

"Our side doesn't really feel like the friendly side, does it? And friendly fire is still deadly fire. I have always been on the winning side, and I am not sure if this is the winning side, any more," James said.

"Aren't you afraid that we might be selling our collective souls to the devil, just to win?" Jennifer asked.

"I am more afraid that President Peel may have done that. Everyone asks us what side we are on, but no one asks what side President Peel is on. It certainly doesn't feel like he is on our side," James said.

"All the sides are blurred and polarized," Maria said.

"Yeah, one side has their point of view, just like looking at the Earth rotating above the north end, we see that Earth is rotating counter-clockwise, then we go above the south end, we see Earth rotating clockwise. And really, what difference does it all make. The social system engineers us to fight each other over the stupidest things. We might as well turn away from Earth so we see no spinning, turn back again to face Earth and then draw and shoot the other side faster than they can shoot us, the way all stupid feuds are won. As far as I can see, we are being pushed backwards into some strange feudalism where everyone is feuding all the time. Maybe it is the End Times. The barons and the richest of landlords will be willing to fight to our deaths, so are they really on our side? And if we let them use us for cannon fodder, when the war is over, our names go up on a wall to remind everyone that we once existed, and the wealthy barons are now freer to progress with their own lives, without guilt. So whose side were they really on?" James asked.

"They don't seem to be on our side that is for sure. Instead of broadening our perspective with art, culture, and beautiful music, we are being poisoned by their hate and greed. Just reading President Peel's tweets makes me feel that my future prospects are going to be hopeless. It is we, the younger generation that will actually be getting killed fighting these wars. We are getting killed before we are even old enough to legally drink or vote. And how do we stop this abuse of power, when we have no social or economic power of our own, not even the right to vote? Maybe the war will be won by our side, but what does that matter if we are all dead?" Jennifer asked.

"We win. And sooner or later, all wars are won when one side surrenders to the other side, because they have either run out of resources or are about to. We kill and destroy until the other side surrenders. We bring in immigrants. We promise them citizenship after the war, upon the condition that we actually win the war and have all the applicable treaties signed indicating that we won. So these imported soldiers are highly motivated to win, since they believe winning is the road to a better life. The problem is, the sides are very blurred. Some of the conflicts are between genders, socio-economic classes, races, and countries. If we live long enough the conflicts will soon be fought in outer space," James said.

"So, Mr. Coaltonstone, you are old enough to have seen what happens when wars are over. Are things really much better, than they were before the war?" Jennifer asked.

"Not really. Often things are a lot worse. Once the war is over, we will have a chance to see which society is truly the most civilised. Once we see how the winning side treats the losing side, we can also predict when the next war will start. If the losing side is tormented so much that many of the citizens believe that losing would be worse than death, then we condition millions of people to fight to the death, especially when the next war comes around," James said.

"What do you think we should be doing, then?" Jennifer asked.

"We should be on the winning side. As simple as that. And that seems to be what we are doing. We should be listening to the other side, and not be so quick when dismissing them as if they mean nothing. We should be disguising our intentions and not look too willing to hurt them so we can progress personally. All is fair in love and war, Jennifer, everyone knows that," James replied.

"James, you think what happened to Mathew was fair? He was just living his life, not hurting anyone, and a projectile came out from nowhere, hit him while he was flyking in his own personal path, in his own space. And here we are, left with a huge hole in our lives that only his return will fill," Maria said.

"Mathew is a smart boy and he probably has been injured. What ever happened to him will confuse him, and he might not realize that he is in a war zone," James said.

"If he is injured the Minese might help him, the way they helped Ginger Goodwin. Now that the borders between us and the Minese are being actively regulated by military law and not just by civil law, the boy will have to remain vigilant and remember that truth and justice will always be on his side," James said.

"Mr. Coaltonstone, the international border has always been regulated by military law, civil law and criminal," Jennifer said.

"Now we are at war, it won't be just up to the discretionary power of the current administration to decide what tactic to use when dealing with illegals," James said.

"We also have laws of economics and natural laws, that are going to shape events too, beyond just all these government regulations and manufactured and provoked conflicts," Maria said.

"Yeah, well fear is the greatest force controlling the conduct of the migrant workers. Both the legal and the illegal Minese are being used as cheap labor and both groups are too afraid to report abuses by employers. Both groups treat each other as competitors and even adversaries so they seem more open to the exclusion process than the process, which would unify them as one group. Even when they lose all human rights and are treated like voluntary slaves or even as sub-humans, the ones who can still vote, seem to be voting for President Peel and the Exclusion League," Jennifer said.

"Who told you that, Jennifer," James asked. "The fake news?"

"President Peel says it all the time. Why do you hire undocumented workers, Mr. Coaltonstone? You do or did, didn't you? Jennifer asked.

"I can't compete without them, because everyone else is hiring them, too. And that is exactly what I am saying. It is about being on the winning side. Those people come over here, treated like shit..." James said.

"James really, you are talking to a child," Maria said.

"I am sorry, Jennifer, if I offended you in any way," James said.

"No offence meant, no offence taken, Sir," Jennifer said.

"Good for you, child. What I was saying, or meant to say," James said as he winked at Maria, "is that the illegals risk everything to be on the side that is winning. They don't care about politics, or documents, all that they want is a better life. Now that the Exclusion League hard liners have taken control, we are being defined as either the Homeland side or the Enemy side. In reality, sides, like everything else is all relative, Jennifer," James said.

"You mean like when you see Earth's rotation above the North Pole spin counter-clockwise, but when someone else sees the Earth spinning above the South Pole clockwise, they start arguing and fighting with each other, as if there is a right side and a wrong side," Jennifer said.

"Exactly, the entire process is relative to where one is standing. Just like war, you might not like the people you are standing closest to, but if they can see something the way you see it, you just automatically feel like you can relate to them. And the foggy war atmosphere that blurs the boundaries between the two sides, calling them good side and bad side, causes mishaps such as the 'friendly fire' which killed Mathew. A child is shot out of the sky while flyking by our side, and we still fear the other side more. It is as if one side reflects the other side, and we never can get through the mirror of distortions that acts even more divisive than that horrible war-wall between Mina and ourselves?" James said.

"What are these wars usually about, Mr. Coaltonstone?" Jennifer asked.

"It is about pecking orders. The old men on each side sending their young men to fight to their deaths or until one side surrenders," James said.

"It couldn't be that simple. President Peel seems to be pushing us so back into time, when we had no allies, and where our economy was pre-industrial revolution. It makes sense for an oligarch to do that to a country It is all about centralizing wealth for a few by making things so expensive hardly anyone will have a surplus to much of anything but survive," Jennifer said.

"If we tried to look deeper than who gets what, and who wins what, we see people on both sides being told who they are and what they are fighting for. We are never really told what the objective is, besides winning of course. Our lives are no longer our own during wartime. Sometimes politicians cut taxes to the bone and try to make up the deficit by introducing tariffs when importing foreign products. Then the new tariffs cause a trade war and the new trade war triggers a new set of hardships. Desperation leads to new conflicts and resentments passed down from generation to generations and could go on for decades. Some wars are fought on the battlefield and others are fought in the financial district and Main Street. While the wars escalate, the soldiers are told who they are and what they must do, to be promoted to a higher rank and pay scale. In the end, no one seems to know what we are fighting for. We know we must win, at all costs. Nobody really tells us anything more than winning this war is everything. Someone starts killing, the other side starts killing, everyone starts killing, but the war doesn't just happen some place far away. We at home become opposing cultures, taking sides and clashing with each other," James said.

"And sometimes we just don't belong on any side," Jennifer said.

"One disaster after another pulls us into so many different directions. And it seems this chaos goes along with the end justifies the means. And in the end there will be a generation, which will be pulled into the abyss of the greatest disaster of all, we just don't know when that disaster will be. Every generation thinks the disasters are so bad, this must be the end, but it isn't, and then a new generation comes along. We are told that the End Times are near, so we don't plan for our future and our family's future. Each generation seems to face the same fear. And Mathew was dismissed by those fools as nothing more than just an unidentified flying object, and then they shot him," Maria said.

"Mathew was identifiable. His phone signals could have identified him to the G.O.D. bots," Jennifer said.

"During wartime, our very existence hangs on the edge at all times. Mathew was not the kind of child who was able to stay on guard for too long," Maria said.

"I think someone at the top is covering something up, that is what I mean about not knowing which side is the good side," Jennifer said.

"We are told war is all about sides, good sides and bad sides. Then we wake up and the past is now behind us and the future is in front of us and that is when we realize that all the sides get blurred. And then we get back to where it all began, we all just wanted to belong and do the right thing, but as the war continues, it is less clear what the right side is but what side we are on was never a choice. We just land up on the side that we are situated on, and we do what we are told or we get accused of treason, and these days that accusation could get published on Twitter," James said.

"You make it sound so simple sort of like the way Mrs. Watson predicts the weather. She predicts it better than all the weather channels put together," Jennifer said as she changed David's diaper.

"War is all about contradictions. Sides are blurred, people stop caring, and sometimes they even wear the message on their back that they don't care," Maria explained. "A lot of people lie to each other, sometimes they say one thing, and wear the polar opposite on their back. Some cry themselves to sleep but the pain wakes up when they wake up."

"You both sound like you are against this war," Jennifer said.

"We are, but what we think about the war, doesn't matter," James said.

"Can you actually predict who is going to win?" Jennifer asked.

"Predicting human behavior is near impossible when you are predicting what one person might do. Whoever wins, is usually the side that doesn't give up, first. Predicting what a hundred people might do is much easier. It is hard to predict when one person might desert. It is easier to predict when a hundred people might desert" James said.

"What about all that weaponized anger? You know when you get short changed in a store, and they refuse to even acknowledge that you had spoken, then one clerk tells the other clerk that you are mental so they don't have to serve people like that? But you know the whole situation is manufactured, so they can rip you off. I think war is the same process. It doesn't seem to matter which side you are on, people treat you like the enemy just by default. It didn't matter that Mathew, Jethro and Bill were technically on the same side, Mathew got shot anyway," Jennifer said.

"I never get short changed because I use a credit card," James said.

"I wish I had a credit card?" Jennifer said.

"I can get you a credit card, Jennifer," James offered.

"No, Jennifer you don't want a credit card," Maria interjected.

"Yes Jennifer, you do," James interjected back. "In the real world, Jennifer you will find that whoever has the power is right. You might count your change one way, but the cashier may count it another, and you know it is just like the way they round the cost and everything to the nearest nickel, you know perfectly well all those rounding errors add up, and over a lifetime, big time. The probabilities are part of what is known and part of what needs to be known and with a bit of luck can be guessed. The better you are at guessing what is unexplained but is nevertheless real, creates luck. The balance between what is fixed and what is variable is not always obvious. Our existence will matter more to people in power when we have a good credit rating. There are so many unknowns we face every day, Jennifer but having good credit makes life easier," James said.

"Why would you want to get into debt just to belong?" Maria said.

"When Mathew was around I always felt like I belonged because I was loved," Jennifer said.

"Jennifer, you must adapt to the world the way is now. The weather patterns are getting more and more violent and unpredictable and so are people. A person with a good credit rating has proof that he or she is reliable in a world that has gone amuck," James explained.

"Do you mean weather related real clouds or weather related fake clouds? Jennifer asked.

"All clouds are real, Jennifer. Some are just feeding from different sources that is all. A cloudburst is a cloud bursting with real, beautiful water," James said. "Channeling that water into water stores such as reservoirs or huge water towers doesn't have to be a hit or miss enterprise, especially when I am in charge. That water could be piped or shipped all over the world to places that need water. Being a rainmaker is not such a bad thing to be, if it is for the good of peoplekind and engineered by talented and gifted people," James said.

"We were reading in school, the other day that cloud seeding could be even done unintentionally by airplanes. When cloud droplets float around jet propellers and tips of airplane wings, the droplets can freeze and even form hailstones," Jennifer said.

"I am not surprised," Maria said. "These sudden storms always scare me. Especially when I am flyking under angry sounding clouds that are discharging lightning bolts," Maria said.

"Make sure you don't tell my mother we were flyking in this weather," Jennifer said.

"I won't lie to your mother, Jennifer, but I won't go out of my way to mention it either. We just happened to get lucky and were able to flyke around the darkest part of that cloudburst," Maria said.

"That cloudburst seemed fake to me," Jennifer said.

"Still a lot of water came out of that cloud. The wind tore down a lot of trees, which would have been devastating for whoever got caught in the storm's path. I bet if that flock of birds could speak they would probably would have told us how lucky we are to have shelter," Maria said.

"I wish someone or something could tell us where Mathew is. I have this gut feeling that Mathew is still alive and is in serious trouble, and he is fighting with all his might just to survive," Jennifer said.

"I get the same feeling. As long as Mathew is alive, he will fight as hard as he can, so that one day he will find his way home. I also get a gut feeling that Jethro and Bill are hiding something, I can just feel it. No one could be stupid enough to mistake a flyker for a drone. I think they shot him down on purpose because he was taking photographs," Maria said. "My guess is they don't want anyone or anything to be taking photographs near their military assets. It was Bill who blew up the whale under Jethro's direction, so we are assuming it was Bill who shot Mathew under Jethro's direction but Jethro and

Bill are refusing to speak to us. Neither of them will say a word."

"After Mathew saw the whale get blown up, he wanted to help the whales so much. And he believed that his photographs could make a difference," Jennifer said.

"Are there any witnesses?" Jennifer asked.

"Not really, the crew won't speak up either. Most of the activities, the crew are involved in are classified as 'MOST SECRET' and are performed in the boat's black room. Anyone, who betrays such secrets, is shot in the forehead. As far as I know these meetings are never recorded," James explained.

"Why is that?" Jennifer asked. "Jethro and Bill get to play God with people's lives, in this case Mathew's and no one can do anything about it?"

"They can't be fired. I tried to fire them," James said.

"Why not?" Jennifer asked.

"I yelled at them that they were fired and then they went to the Brotherhood and are now only talking to us through their lawyer, Muni Bugden," James confirmed.

"Their lawyer is complaining that they were under severe stress at the time of the shooting. And they are both mixed up and can't remember who did what. To make a long story short, the Brotherhood has been successful in stopping us firing them," James explained.

"James, do you think Mathew took an incriminating photo of Bill and Jethro?" Maria asked.

"It is possible, isn't it?" Jennifer said as looked at James.

"Anything is possible," James replied.

"And knowing Mathew, if he could have, he would have taken a picture and maybe even sold his pictures to Jackson so he could distribute them to a wider audience, and help the whales by donating to the charities designed to make a difference to sea life. Jackson often bought Mathew's photos, and Mathew often donated his money to 'Save the Whales and all Sea Creatures Society'," Jennifer said.

"I didn't know that, and I didn't know that Mathew had such a special love interest," James said while winking.

"The more Mathew flyked over the sea, the more he grew to love the sea creatures that he could see jumping in the air. Mathew loved this world and could still the beauty in it," Jennifer said.

"Jethro and Bill probably would have shot Mathew down on purpose if they had seen him taking photos of them, knowing those two," James said.

"If those hillbilly thugs deliberately shot Mathew down, they should be hung from the nearest tree," Jennifer said.

"I agree," James said.

"Jennifer and James, really, we always have to remember that terrible errors of judgment are often outcomes of an impoverished cultural environment. And whenever people like Bill and Jethro are making split-second decisions, who knows what horrible unintended effects will occur," Maria said.

"And the intended effects are even worse," James said.

"You can say that again," Jennifer said.

"James, you hired those fools," Maria added.

"I know. I make it a policy to never hire anyone smarter than myself," James replied sheepishly.

'Why would anyone ever hire those redneck spies?" Jennifer asked.

"Don't ever underestimate those two, Jennifer. I wish I fired them after they blew up the whale," James said.

"I wish you did too," Maria and Jennifer said at the same time.

"Why didn't you? You must have known how dangerous those two could be when armed to the teeth?" Maria asked.

"Because I just assumed that James and Jethro had made an honest mistake. But there is no excuse for making two terrible mistakes; first blowing up a whale and then shooting down Mathew, that kind of behavior is insanity," James replied.

"Typical behavior of the End Days," Maria said.

"I believe I will make the future a lot brighter than that with my hyper-loop peace connector. I believe that vision has to be noble for our deeds to be progressive. And hiring those two yahoos to spy on innocent people, was the worst mistake of my life," James said.

"But after that, you must have known they were fools. If you hadn't kept them on your payroll, they wouldn't have been armed to the teeth and in a position to shoot down Mathew," Jennifer said.

"Jennifer, we can't hang people just because they are fools," Maria scolded.

"But we should, if they are murderers, because they could murder again," Jennifer said.

"Well the biggest fool in this situation is the one that gave those two such deadly power in the first place. I am the one that will have to live with that mistake for the rest of my life," James said.

"Our lives are messed up because of all the bad decisions you older people make for us. Many of these bad decisions are made in secret, and we won't be getting access to those classified documents until we are as old as you are now, if we even live that long. Mathew, if he is dead, died way too young. It just isn't fair. And then there is all the garbage hand me downs you expect us to wear and the moldy tomatoes that get shoved into discount bags in grocery stores. We are doomed. Mathew is possibly dead, and wasn't even sixteen yet. And you old people, seem to live forever," Jennifer said.

"Jennifer, what do you expect from life?" James asked.

"Nothing," Jennifer replied.

"Exactly. And I, my dear child expect and demand greatness and scowl until I get it," James said.

"No one kicks you down the way we get kicked, down, watched and scrutinized. It is almost like the culture of manufactured despair is meant to make the ones feeling the most cornered wanting to commit suicide," Jennifer said. "I think that is why Mathew loved to flyke in the open sky, because that was the only time he actually felt free."

"Hindsight is a wonderful thing, it lets people believe they could have come up with a great idea as they reverse engineer a product in their mind, they probably say anyone could have done that. Which is not the point. The point is without high expectations, it is almost impossible to get back up after getting knocked down during all the hard knocks life dishes out. Hindsight has a lot more advantage than the foresight needed to be the first to come up with an idea or product. Hindsight feels almost as good as foreplay," James said with a wicked grin.

"James, you are talking to a child," Maria scolded again.

"Mrs. Watson, I am not a child. I am old enough to be a cadet and I am technically old enough to kill. I am just not old enough to vote," Jennifer said.

"Jennifer, if you had been old enough, would have you voted for me, or for President Peel and his Exclusion League?"

"Talk about a loaded question?" Maria said, trying to make this moment less uncomfortable for Jennifer.

"I would have voted for the Green Party," Jennifer replied.

"Joking aside," James began to say.

"I am not joking Mr. Coaltonstone. I think there is a lot more harmony in nature's economy than the artificial economics which dominates the Tut territory. And I miss Mathew so much," Jennifer said.

"I can't apologize enough for hiring Jethro and Bill. I had no idea how stupid, reckless and dangerous Jethro and Bill would be," James explained.

"But it is wartime, Mr. Coaltonstone, isn't that the way everyone seems to be?" Jennifer asked.

"Yes, that is the way everyone seems to be reckless and angry. People like Jethro and Bill follow their own hunches and fears, just like the exclusion league does. Regardless of anyone else, they shout and ask questions later, or more correctly, others are left asking the questions. Men like Jethro and Bill survive war after war and kids like my grandson are made casualties of war as it was nothing," Maria said as she fought back tears.

"I don't think it is that simple Maria. I think men like Jethro and Bill don't realize how stupid and dangerous they are, but I should have known," James replied.

"We don't even know who did the shooting. This situation is just horrible, and because of all this confusion, my bet is both of them will be walking, allowed to keep their jobs. The G.O.D. bots won't care because how can they? Originally Bill said that he was the one who blew up the whale but according to the media counts that I heard, it was Jethro, so who can we believe?" Maria asked.

"The scary thing is, Jethro and Bill are supposed to be on our side in this war," Jennifer said as she clung on to the bible she had on her lap.

"The G.O.D. bots are probably referring to Mathew as collateral damage as we speak," Maria replied.

"Why did you hire such stupid men, Mr. Coaltonstone?" Jennifer asked.

"I don't usually hire people smarter than myself," James began to say before Maria interjected.

"You mean, the more Jethro and Bill know and understand about your organization, the more power they could actually take from you? That is really scary because they will always be controlled by their negative bias which makes them super stupid," Jennifer said.

"I think James was trying to say that he hires people who are not as smart as he is because he wants all the power to himself," Maria explained.

"Of course that is not what I meant. Jennifer, I notice you have a bible on your lap, why?" James asked probably trying to change the subject as soon as possible.

"The words soothe the soul James, and we need as much soothing as we can get at the moment," Maria explained. "We also find playing our etherplayers soothing."

"I suppose that is why so many people follow President Peel's tweets. For some strange reason, they find them soothing," James said.

"At the moment, I need soothing all the time, but I certainly would not turn to President Peel's tweets. He does not represent me, I don't relate to him as my president on any level at all. I can't believe that Mathew is gone. We had great plans and all I have left is this huge hole in my life and heart, while Jethro and Bill are free to live their own lives as if nothing happened," Jennifer said.

"I feel the same way as Jennifer does. The hole in my life and heart just ache," Maria added.

"I have to believe that some part of Mathew still lives," Jennifer said.

"We both do. And part of Mathew will always be alive. The part that is invisible to the eye but is still there, surrounding us," Maria said.

"You mean the electro-magnetic force that makes our etherplayers sing, and make the clouds roar out their thunder and lightning? That force of nature?" Jennifer asked.

"Exactly! The world is going crazy with paranoia and greed. Stealth drones are taking over the skies and the G.O.D. bots fill their data banks with personal information about us, as if we were the things and they were the humans. It is anyone's guess if those huge warehouses that need vast amounts of channeled energy to run, will even be here if this war lasts for twenty years. Strange that they call their huge storage facility the Cloud. The world is being turned into something hard, ruthless and soulless and no wonder the Earth's spin is slowing down," Maria said.

"Hasn't his war, in some form or other been going on for over twenty years already? Someone always finds something to fight about. If it is not one thing, then the Exclusion League will find another," Jennifer said.

"Bill and Jethro should have never have been given the power they now have. It is much easier to hire members of the Brotherhood than it is to fire them. And their power could make us all casualties of war, sooner or later. It is sort of my fault," James said.

"Sort of?" Maria said, mockingly.

"Do you always hire such stupid men because you want your employees to always be less intelligent than you are?" Jennifer asked.

"It isn't that simple," James said defensively.

"Sure it is. There are people who do creative things for a living and others do destructive things like marginalize others less advantaged," Jennifer said.

"What I meant to say was that it is hard to find someone smarter than me to start with. Finding someone smarter than me would have been a rare event. Everyone prefers to be smarter than the hired help," James said.

"Help? You call Jethro and Bill help? I call those two a curse on mankind," Maria said.

"Peoplekind dear, Peoplekind," James replied.

"James, Mathew was probably murdered by those two fools that you hired, and you are making jokes?"

"I am sorry Maria. Things are very complicated. The skies are saturated with unidentified flying objects. Shooting objects down are split second decisions. What happens if we lost the war because we were too slow to shoot our enemies down, so they shoot us all down first? Can you even imagine living in a world where the ruling language was no longer English?

"James, please don't patronize me. The last thing we need is another black cloud building up next to all the other black clouds surrounding us. It is just a matter of time before all the black clouds rain on all of us," Maria said.

"I understand, dear," James said.

"Will you stop calling me dear and start taking me seriously," Maria kicked herself for actually sounding as if she was begging.

"I am sorry Maria, if I offended you in anyway. We are on the same side," James said.

"Jethro and Bill are technically on our side too and look how far that is getting us," Maria said.

"Bill and Jethro's victims are also on our side, and the way we deny the tragedy which has happened to Mathew makes me sick to my stomach," Jennifer said.

"The problem is never as simple as what side a person is on. Jethro and Bill are officially on our side but that does not make their friendly fire any less deadly," James said.

"The problem is that the members of the G.O.D. administration don't apologize when they make mistakes, or after they have turned someone's life upside down. It is really hard to know who to trust, who is going to make all this better," Maria said.

"Maria, I am on your side. I may not be perfect but I loved Mathew like a son. I have a huge hole in my life ever since Mathew has been reported missing. All I am saying is during wartime a person might not just get killed by an enemy that he cannot see, but often by someone on his own side who doesn't see him. Sometimes it is a mistake, other times it is by design," James said.

"What do you mean, Mr. Coaltonstone?" Jennifer asked.

"You remember the story of Caesar and Brutus, right?"

"Of course," Jennifer replied.

"With great knowledge comes great power, but who you know and trust poses risks too. There is no greater hurt felt when someone abuses and betrays your trust, especially when it puts the entire republic at risk. Often the people closest to you have the greatest power to hurt you. Usually staying disengaged and uninvolved, especially during the fogginess of wartime, protects people. Familiarity feels safe. Usually the foggier the situation is, and the riskier it really is. Familiarity gives a sense of belonging, but when it all comes crashing down around you, you feel like you belong nowhere. When the situation is so foggy, and no one can see clearly, that is usually the time when innocent people go missing, or worse, turn up dead in a field somewhere," James said.

"Can we please tone down this conversation a notch? I am trying to stay positive and hopeful. There must be something positive I can focus on. James, please tell me that there is something positive to focus on," Maria asked.

"I think our love for Mathew will give us the strength we will need to carry on," Jennifer said.

"How do you know what you felt for Mathew, was really love. Whenever you saw Mathew, Jennifer, did you feel a feeling like a lightning bolt taking over your entire body?" James asked.

"James, really," Maria scolded.

"Of course I did, and it was wonderful, Mr. Coaltonstone, but I know if we never give up, we will find him," Jennifer said.

"Maria, why do you think people are lining up to buy young blood at fifteen thousand dollars a shot?" James asked.

"Do you do that, Mr. Coaltonstone?" Jennifer asked.

"Of course not," James lied.

"My guess is that Mathew was just flyking around and taking photos of whatever he fancied. Mathew was always at his happiest when he was flyking around taking photos of interesting and beautiful things. He seemed to get intoxicated by all the beautiful nature flying near him and probably didn't even realize that Jethro and Bill's submarine was still nearby. When Mathew got hit, he probably had no idea by what, or why," Jennifer speculated.

"I just don't believe, someone, and their flyking equipment could disappear in thin air, without a trace," Maria said.

"Mathew was a big boy. It was amazing how graceful he was when he was flyking," James said.

"James, stop talking about him as if he were dead," Maria pleaded.

"It is hard not to. He told me over and over again how close he felt to his dad when he was flyking beneath the heavens," James said.

"James, please. I have to believe my grandson is still alive," Maria said.

"He was my stepson, and I want to believe that he is alive too," James said.

"I remember Mathew feeling such joy and energy the moment I bought him his first flyke. It was like he was a kid again. That tortured look on his face, which appeared after his father was killed, started to disappear. I thought a part of Mathew was going to be lost forever after his dad was killed by that horrible boss bot," Maria said.

"Maria, it was proven in court that it was human error that killed Mathew's father," James said.

"Proven how? By only voices of the appointed?"

"Come on you guys. We have to tone it down," Jennifer said.

"I have to go, I am sorry to cut this conversation short. I have to work on my rail project. I am sure that I will bump into you ladies soon," James said as he closed the door behind him.

"Mathew loved flyking and being so close to his dad and of course I loved being so close to my son too," Maria said as her voice began to crack.

"I get really negative vibes whenever I think of those two morons. Jethro and Bill seem to have no common sense. First they blow up a whale, then they might have blown up Mathew, and they are still allowed to roam freely under the sea in that nuclear tin can," Jennifer said.

"Do you think Mr. Coaltonstone has anything to do with Mathew's disappearance?" Jennifer asked.

"No, not intentionally anyway. I am sure he feels responsible since he hired Jethro and Bill, but I know he is trying his hardest to get them fired, but they are protected by the Brotherhood," Maria replied.

"Sometimes I wonder if Mr. Coaltonstone is taking some kind of anti-aging compound. At times he seems to have loads of energy, almost too much, for an old person, then other times he looks like he is fighting off the sleep of death," Jennifer said.

"I notice that too, but I know James thinks the world of Mathew, and would never harm him, intentionally anyway," Maria said.

"Every time I see Mr. Coaltonstone change from acting young to old, I think about all the young blood being smuggled into the country from Mina. I read about it all the time on line," Jennifer said.

"It is hard to know what James is taking but I am certain that he would never harm Mathew. I am also certain that James would pay someone a pretty penny to kill anyone who has hurt Mathew in any way for whatever reason. I am sure Jethro and Bill are fearing for their lives as we speak," Maria said.

CHAPTER 6:

A Major Discovery under Cold Feet Mountain

March 18th 2031, around 10:00 AM: "Welcome back, all loyal viewers and to all my new viewers, a very special welcome. As you can see we are under Coalton in a wonderful magical place, it is so new the underground lake doesn't even have a name yet. The shiny, psychedelic fish are real. They light up in the dark, swim around glow in the dark water mushrooms and have teeth, only adding more magic and intrigue to this newly found, wonderful place," Dianne announced to the world while Jackson held his camera in place, scanning and zooming,

"My moles have told me that this place must have always existed since it just couldn't have just appeared overnight. This portion of the cave is directly under Coalton Two so it is not clear if it is publically owned or owned by the Big Seven Coal Group mining super power. It is only an access to the strange underground cave system, which appeared under Coalton Two and right next door to the Coalton Mine under Cold Feet Mountain. Speculation has it that when part of Cold Feet Mountain came tumbling town on top of Coalton Two, which happened three days ago, on March 15th, at around 5:45 AM. The cause of the greatest slide where around ninety people, just a rough estimate are buried along with the content of only Coalton Bank, is still under investigation. The formation of this wonderful cave is mostly limestone, similar to the rock which form Cold Feet Mountain. There are many narrow tunnels, which would be a real chore to climb and squeeze, even though the caving enthusiasts among my loyal viewers are going to want to explore this gem of caves. Back to you Steve," Dianne said as she gave the signal for Jackson to turn off the camera and mike.

"Jackson, keep the light on. Let's see if we can find anything," Dianne ordered.

"What are you expecting to find, don't forget the fish in here are carnivores," Jackson warned.

"Well, we don't know that," Dianne replied.

"What do you think they have teeth for, to eat seaweed? Maybe they eat their young?" Jackson asked.

"Jackson, please, I am trying to find something," Dianne said.

"I am just saying, we need to be careful, especially if there is something in here that doesn't want to be found," Jackson said.

"Shh," Dianne ordered.

"What are you doing with that stethoscope?" Jackson asked.

"What does it look like I am doing? I am trying to listen behind this rock," Dianne explained while sounding irritated. "Jackson Shh, I think I can hear banging and children crying."

"Are you sure it not just a bunch of bats. You know, Di, if something is going on, we shouldn't be here alone. This is a creepy enough place where something could be going on, it would be going on here, no doubt. We need to get out of here, quickly. We can come back here later, maybe with more people, or at least with more eyes and ears," Jackson advised.

CHAPTER 7:

Who Is Manipulating the Weather?

March 18th 2031, around 12:00 PM: "What do you mean this extreme weather is my fault?" James Coaltonstone said sounding more hurt that angry with Dianne for insinuating such a thing. "Weaponizing weather is not my style. How would I even go about doing such a thing?"

"It was you who wanted to nuke the Arctic ice so you could mine for what might be below it," Dianne said.

"That is different. I had good intentions. I wanted to free the wealth from below, put idle men back to work in the mines, and make a difference to mankind by being the first to build a link between Eurasia and North America," James said.

"What about the pending land deals and mineral rights with the natives?" Jackson asked.

"And all that protected parkland that is now being reevaluated," Dianne added.

"Who isn't native? What in nature isn't beautiful," James retorted.

"James, how did you manage to privatize such a lucrative portion of the Arctic? What about the natives who say their claims have been pending for over a century, and are now being ignored? What about them?" Dianne asked.

"What about them? Wealth comes from the ground. It doesn't grow on trees. I have to spend a lot of my own money before I can find veins rich with beautiful coal. One of the best presents I was given, as a child, was a lump of coal, even though my mouthy cousin, Lance, kept telling me I didn't understand the message that getting coal for Christmas was not a good thing. It sure is a great thing to get if you are cold, or if you want to cook something to eat, or if you want to fire up the engines of the world. I am managing to live longer than my idealistic, numskull of a cousin did, and so what does that tell you?" James said.

"Yes, I remember Lance, he tried to rescue Ginger Goodwin from Mine Five, but miraculously the Minese found a way to rescue Ginger first. He also left a legacy of vertical farm-towers and water towers that are providing food to feed and water millions of people living in drought conditions. I have no idea what happened to Lance, he just seemed to have disappeared," Dianne said as she remembered Ginger Goodwin's rescue, as if it happened yesterday.

"I don't know what happened to Lance either and I don't care. I never talk to that side of my family. We have always had differences of opinion. Those farm and water towers bring down the cost of food by increasing food security, which makes suppliers in our country less money," James said.

"You are kidding? Right?" Jackson asked.

"I certainly am not. It makes sense that the Minese miners would find Ginger first, but those fancy vertical farm-towers could lower cost of food on a global scale, which doesn't make sense to me at all," James said.

"You would let people die of mass starvation so you can keep food prices high?" Dianne asked.

"I am not the bad guy here. Letting people die of mass starvation culls the population and it is much cheaper than killing them in warfare. It is the way it is meant to be. We don't have enough land to feed the globe," James said.

"Unless we build vertical farm tires up, into the sky, the way Lance was doing," Jackson said.

"The Minese miners know my mines and my tunnels better than they know the hand that feeds them. And that is exactly why I am saying we need more workers like the Minese, not less. Lance was trying to make it safer for the rescue team and his plan was to widen the ventilation shaft in Section E to make it wide enough so that Ginger could use the ventilation shaft as an escape shaft," James said.

"Those Minese appear to know entrances and exits to different places through the mines, mountains and tunnel systems that go beyond what most of the Buynese will ever know," Dianne said. "I heard, from one of my moles that the Minese miners hooked up Ginger to an oxygen tanks with back up batteries, and laid him on a stretcher. They carried him from the Safety Chamber and used the shaft lift to bring him out to the surface in Mine Eight, which is not a functioning coal, mine at all, but an underground hemp plantation," Dianne said.

"I haven't heard of such fake news, in all my life. At one point we were considering opening a Mine Eight, but we decided to move our operation to Coalton Two, and Mine Eight doesn't even exist. And we certainly wouldn't be growing hemp in a mine. Lance tried his best to help Ginger, but the Minese are just faster and more fearless moving around underground while ignoring hazards," James said.

"Lance Diamond was one of the last gentlemanly barons, as far as I know. His death is still clouded over by mystery and dead ends. Whenever we try to find anything out about what happened people keep telling us to be aware of the Black Diamond curse, which is said to be worse than the Kennedy Curse," Jackson said.

"The problem with those curses is that until the debt which caused the curse in the first place is paid back, the curse is passed down from generation to generation including members of the extended family, as legend has it anyway," James said.

"Ginger refused to respond to the call of duty, when his number came up. It just shows you how human kindness is able to bond people, even during times of war. Kindness seems to be one of the few forces that seems to defy the power the Exclusion League I holding over Tut. Excluding people who were kind to you, pulls at the heartstrings," Dianne said.

"Ginger was an outlier, which is the best that I can say about him," James said.

"How true is the rumor that has been floating around for decades, that Ginger was your biological son and was taken away shortly after birth and given to the Goodwin family, after your only true love, Marie-Rose, died in child birth? Then when Ginger was still in his teens, the Goodwin family was killed driving on the Tut Island Highway," Dianne enquired.

"Just more fake news from the failing PPZ, which is starting to make me very angry. And if I am ever asked about family business that is not any of your business again, I will refuse to give you any more interviews, Dianne. And that includes you too, Jackson," James said.

"I am sorry if Dianne offended you in any way," Jackson said as he winked at Dianne. "We were hoping that you could tell us more about Deep Coal, who or what Deep Coal is. The data that Ginger Goodwin was able to mine from Mine Five, was the closest we have ever come to non-biased facts," Jackson said as James sighed.

"That is quite the stretch, even for you types from the failing PPZ. Deep Coal was an illegal just like any other undocumented person on Tut Island is. Deep Coal was not authorized to share propriety information owned by the Big Seven Coal Group. And the moment Ginger Goodwin refused to fight the illegals and vagrants he became one of them, and then he was destined to be purged," James explained.

"To many, Ginger Goodwin was a hero and a friend," Jackson replied.

"Anyway, I have signed a binding contract with the G.O.D. ..." James said.

"You signed a contract with the Exclusion League? Are you going to condone the outlawing of human kindness so everyone of draftable age is war ready?" Dianne asked.

"Hold on James, I have a couple of questions about Ginger Goodwin and the draft. Was Ginger drafted because you and your cronies were out to get him even though he was not medically fit for military service? Ginger appeared to be suffering from black lung, after working in the mine, and had bad teeth," Dianne asked.

"What kind of question is that? Not that I should have expected better from the fake news makers of the failing PPZ," James said.

"The second question is why is a judge agreeing to hear a test case on whether the military draft lottery, in this terrible war against the Minese, may not be random at all? My moles have revealed that respected statisticians are discovering that the military lottery draft picks based on late in the year birthday dates, which include December of course, the month when Ginger Goodwin was born, defy the odds and the law of probabilities. In short the military draft lottery appears to have been rigged, especially as it relates to Ginger Goodwin's case," Dianne said.

"I am not answering any more questions from you Dianne. I refuse to have my time hijacked," James said.

"I wanted to get your opinion about President Peel, his Exclusion League backers and this war, many refer to as a race war," Dianne said.

"I have a very important announcement that I must make and whatever criticism I have of President Peel, I keep to myself," James replied.

"So you do not agree with President Peel and the Exclusion League backers?" Dianne asked.

"What would you have me say, Dianne. I want to overthrow the president because I think he is insane and this war is stupid and stifling my efforts. Then you fake news types could print that I am a traitor. With all joking aside, I will ignore your rude question and continue with my informal announcement. There are two things we don't discuss in polite society, race and money. I have signed a contract. In return for the compensation I receive, I will be working side by side with my Minese and other international colleagues. We are building a very great and beautiful Bering Strait Rail-Tube-Bridge Peace Complex, which will connect Eurasia with North America and by default South America," James explained.

"But we are at war with Mina," Jackson protested.

"No, we are at war with the Minese government. We are not at war with the Minese people, especially not the billionaires. One day, when my hyper-loop rail service is made public we will have many checkpoints. There will be botcops, both public and private, staying tirelessly on guard for the real free world. There will be dronecops, which will be programmed to fly wherever the United International Authorities dictate," James said, rather pleased with himself that he managed to negotiate such a great deal with such powerful authorities for himself and the Big Seven Coal Group.

"You are proposing a global and secret surveillance program, during a time of war between races?" Dianne asked.

"What better time is there? Wartime is the perfect time to introduce such a program," James said.

"None of this makes any sense to me. What you are suggesting, contradicts all that we know about economics and human behavior that has always worked so well in the free world," Jackson said.

"Really? You think President Peel's regime respects; life, liberty and the pursuit of happiness? I care about those things, a lot," James said.

"What you are proposing works best for countries that live behind walls, like the iron curtain," Jackson said.

"So what side of the wall do you think my stepson might be on, if he is still alive?" James asked.

"I don't know," Dianne said.

"President Peel's war-wall is a waste of money and aggravates people and blocks the view. Only authorized bots are able to see over the wall. Why not complain about that? Jackson, both you and Dianne have a right to your opinions, and I have a right to argue to the death to defend my opinions, my property and my future prospects," James said.

"Is fighting to the death to defend an opinion, really necessary or even civilized?" Jackson asked.

"There have always been foggy wars. Walls can't keep the fog out. The foggy wars' greatest by-products, besides the chaos, are the great global metropoles and the smug old men who run them, behind their portable security fencing that they take everywhere they go," Dianne said.

"We need to continue with world trade but how can we, when we are being engineered to distrust each other? We need to keep our markets friendly, sustainable and open for business. We need to export and import salt products to keep the roads of the world ice-free. We need to import and export our oil, gas and coal to keep the engines of the world running. We need to import laborers, if we want to continue keeping the engines of Tut, fired up, so to speak. Our Metropolis' need for energy channeling products is accelerating. Our energy needs have never been higher in Tut history. We must import energy and consumer products when we are unable to produce these products economically at home. So no wonder why we are importing so much more than we are exporting. We would be fools to blame other countries for that. We should be thanking those countries for helping us to live the way we do. It is not like we don't export a lot. We just import more than we export because it is more economical to do so. Our Metropolis needs its roads and sidewalks cleared of ice, more often than ever before. Some days it is far too cold for humans to progress, without heat or deicing vehicles, planes, roads and sidewalks. Other days it is far too hot for any kind of work to be done without the continuous hum of air conditioners and fans running in the background," James said.

"And you haven't even mentioned tires melting as they roll down our roadways and our electricity wires melting during one heat wave after another. Do you have an opinion on what might be causing such horrific events, Mr. Coaltonstone?" Dianne asked.

"I really don't know," James replied.

"Are you denying that melting the Arctic ice to find all this new oil, gas and coal will flood towns, homes and most likely contribute to global warming?" Dianne asked.

"Why do you keep changing the subject, Dianne? Why didn't you ever ask Tut Hydro to explain why they were flying around with cloud seeding equipment the day before the great Buzzard Creek flood? Why didn't you ask about the sudden torrential rains that appeared from nowhere? That disaster appeared to be the work of what Jennifer likes to call fake clouds. Property was damaged, crops were ruined, and homeless people camping nearby, apparently drowned in their sleep," James said.

"We have asked Tut Hydro about their role in that flood, and they refuse to offer us an explanation," Dianne replied. "We asked about what happened to the people who drowned in the flood and we were told they were illegals and deserved to drown, but the CEO threatened to sue me if I quoted him," Dianne said.

"And why didn't you ever ask the Tut Militia about their policy of using cloud seeding to rain-out their political enemies even when those clouds are being created directly above Tut Island? Those politically motivated rain-outs, lacking for a better word, create catastrophic floods, causing billions of dollars in property damage and pose a threat to anyone sleeping under those fake clouds. And while you are at it why don't you ask the militia why they are allowing transients to camp out in the open," James said.

"You know how the militia operate. The members will the G.O.D. bots to purge without asking any questions. The Brotherhood serves only the Tut Metropolis. It is bad enough that Tut Island is treated like a colony, but once the East and the West are physically linked, who knows who will win the power struggle for control. One day we could become a colony for the Minese government. Your crazy plan could backfire on us. And of course we all know that Homeland Security, for the East and for the West, forbid any publication related to the ongoing military strategy. Assuming that there is one," Dianne said.

"Some win and some lose. That is the way of the world. If I wasn't such a winner all I would be is an old man waiting to die, reading President Peel's awful tweets," James replied.

"That is not true," Dianne retorted.

"Dianne, it certainly is true. No one has time for old people unless they still have power and means to elevate themselves from the undignified process of aging," James said.

"Aging is all in the mind, James," Di said.

"Really? You of all people must know how aging will affect your ratings and how seriously you will be taken as you speak," James said.

"Anyway, you can't deny that the Bering Strait Rail-Tube-Bridge Peace Complex connecting Eurasia with North America will be a connector of the greatest ingenuity and beauty. Who would rather spend all that money on war and trade wars, when we could open our markets and minds to a more unified world? Do we stop being first if we let our markets stay open markets. What does being first mean anyway? Innovation keeps us ahead of the race. The moment we stop innovating, we all fall behind. Who cares who falls behind first? The black market, free from tariffs and counter-tariffs could take over. Our challenges, when overcome, will elevate humanity to new historic heights. The future for our young people will be exciting, dynamic and worth living. Young people will have greater choices when it is time for them to decide what path to take and who they will grow to become," James said as he waved his arms. "This is a dream shared by many other great men and women. When I close my eyes, I see a future that is great and wonderful. We have the technology to link Eurasia with the Americas. We can be confident that our technology is able to drain swamps, modify hurricanes and free the wealth trapped below that waste land of ice that gets in the way of everything," James said.

"James, have you forgotten all the disasters that you have been part of and that I have been covering for the PPZ, because it is my job to show the public events that are in the public interest to know?" Dianne asked.

"You talk to me as if my work makes me the enemy, so what does that make you?" James asked.

"Putting all your kidding aside, it is a fact that you have been directly or indirectly involved in one disaster after another. You always seem to come out at the top end though. People I have spoken to personally have lost their homes, their jobs and loved ones due to these disasters that seem to be nothing more than an inconvenience to you," Dianne said.

"So what are you and your crew of fake newsmakers going to accuse me of next? Stealing the rainclouds above Coalton and so I can sell them to California or worse, an enemy theocracy? Would such a scenario even be as bad as the droughts that are plaguing California? Weather is controlled by forces that live above and below man," James said. "To steal the clouds that belong to those forces, is like selling your soul to the devil, it is very ill advised. Very ill advised," James said.

"It wouldn't be the first time unintended consequences took over and grew out of control," Dianne said.

"You were the one who wanted to nuke ice caps so you could mine under them, regardless of who or what could be flooded or how the climate could be affected," Jackson said as he carefully changed David's diaper.

"That little guy sure goes through a lot of diapers. And he is so handsome," James said.

"Don't change the subject, James," Dianne scolded.

"I am not changing the subject. I am preparing for David's entry into the future, his future and Mary's future. All that I am saying is it isn't me who is stealing and seeding clouds. I have no interest in seeding clouds or stealing them. My interest lies in the vast wasteland under all that ice that seems to be taking forever to melt," James said. "I am not even sure that cloud seeding works. Some people swear by it and some people say the risks outweigh the benefits," James said.

"Have you ever thought about renting the Tut Hydro cloud seeding plane and see if you could put out the fire under Pitville?" Dianne asked.

"I think about it for a second or two. The fire is spreading under the ground and probably started at the Buzzard Creek Dump. But once the fire sparks my coal seam beneath, if it hasn't already, I think a newer technology will be needed to put out the underground fire. The early move to Coalton Two was partly a salvage effort on my part and partly just an acceleration of what I had already planned to do. The moving dates were just pushed ahead, slightly. I don't think we have the technology that can stop that fire at its source, unless we rain on it."

"I am sure the fake clouds are being used all the time to modify the weather and put out unofficial fires," Jackson said.

"G.O.D. bots are in charge of weather management, why don't you blame them when things go wrong, instead of me? I dare you to accuse G.O.D.'s bots in one of your newscasts. I know you won't because you know just as much as I know what would happen, G.O.D. bots would be at your door in no time and you would no longer be allowed to broadcast your fake news. There would be no time for due process, which is a waste of time anyway. You would be declared guilty and that it would be it. You would be rotting in jail without dental floss and with nothing much to do but watch your beauty fade in between your shifts in the labor camps. So blame me and my quest to find buried minerals under ice and so we can continue to benefit from the engine of the world stays running and turned on," James said as he jotted down part of the line he just said.

"What are you writing?" Dianne asked.

"The foundation of my new slogan. Imagine Dianne, the engines of the world turned off, no more Facebook, no more media, and no more cash registers ringing in time with the Salvation Army bells ringing in the streets filled with Christmas shoppers rushing around. Without the finite engines of the world powered and running, we would be thrown back into the abyss of feudalism, or worse, slavery and the breakdown of civil society, as we know it. Children would have no childhood and would be turned into cannon fodder at a very young age," James warned.

"Mr. Coaltonstone, we are being turned into cannon fodder at a very young age. The draft lottery is a big deal for people my age. Most of us don't even believe that a race war is legitimate. Most of the kids I know believe that we human beings are a lot more than just machines that can be triggered through sensors that are skin deep. Why should we have to fight a war that we don't even believe in? Eighteen is really young to be drafted and sent to a foreign land. Fighting a war that is hard to understand let alone believe in is a form of slavery. Look how old you are compared to how young I am," Jennifer interrupted.

"Jennifer you just barge in here from nowhere, interrupt this adult conversation I am having with Dianne and Jackson and you know perfectly well that your opinion doesn't matter to the adults in this room," James said.

"Speak for yourself James, Jennifer's autonomy as a human being does matter," Dianne said.

"Thank you," Jennifer said.

"Where did you come from and what did you just say to me, young lady? Don't you know how rude it is to interrupt your elders when they are speaking, regardless of how liberal one of them might be? I won't even mention how disrespectful it is to barge into a room or conversation, without being invited," James scolded.

"Let it go, James," Maria pleaded.

"Don't you wonder how the military draft lottery is going to work? Whose number is going to get called? Who gets to go on with their life? Mathew used to wonder about it all the time. I do too. Now Mr. Peel is going to be tweeting out the entire lottery process to the whole planet, as if it were just another reality show. But kids my age are going to be sent overseas, and some of us will never return home. And Mathew has been shot by friendly fire, which at the end has the same result as enemy fire, but more disappointing, less chance for a medal, less dignified," Jennifer said.

"Don't you women ever shut up?" James asked.

"We just walked in and surprise, surprise, first thing we hear is the voice of oppression. Why don't you listen to Jennifer? Or are you so attached to your grumpy old man routine, you refuse to let it go to get along?" Maria replied.

"Mr. Coaltonstone, I bet you would fight to the death with a child if you ever felt your power was being threatened, wouldn't you?" Jennifer said.

"It would depend," James said. "If it were wartime I would have little choice."

"It is wartime," Jennifer said.

"There you go. Your question is answered," James replied.

"And the new laws that are passed to keep the younger generation out of the actual workforce just drive me crazy. The new law that a person has to either work or go to school, sounds reasonable at first glance, then you realize it is really not offering an entry point to a job, just more student debt. The law also ignores the hardship a higher education is costing and the debt load it creates, especially when so many of the good jobs are being taken over by robots. We are getting stuck in a terrible situation. If I think about it for too long, getting turned into cannon fodder by the older generation, is not the worse option," Jennifer said.

"People are being driven mad with hunger in many countries. We have it good here. The greatest tyrant of all is the beast within, when the beast is about to die under the fate of poverty," James said.

"Events that happen are a process. It is my job to discover the order of the process and share this information with the public," Dianne said.

"And to do what? Sway public opinion to be for or to be against something or someone?" James asked.

"Maybe with a bit of luck we can avoid repeating history," Dianne replied

"More like just profiting from all the fake news related hysteria you broadcast daily for the failing PPZ. You call facts you don't like fake but the reality is that the polar bears are turning to cannibalism to survive. And humans seem to be doing the same, but in a different way. It is frightening and heart breaking. The ice is melting, the lakes, even the ones who are only called great by name are growing and sucking up towns, homes and lives that used to matter to the rest of the world," Jackson said, raising his voice.

"Slander and defamation is not about news, it is about power. Whenever you get everyone worked up you increase your ratings. Why not let the polar bears do what they do in peace?" James asked.

"James you are kidding? Right?" Dianne asked.

"Not really. Whenever there is a tragedy in nature we seek an explanation, an answer, but nature itself is just as tragic as it is beautiful. There are some things that cannot be explained, and other things just don't need to be explained. They just are," James said.

CHAPTER 8:

Who Is Stealing the Clouds?

March 18th 2031, around 12:10 PM: "If birds and bees can do it, so can we," Maria said.

"I am certain of it," James said.

"I wasn't talking to you James, I was talking to Jennifer," Maria replied.

"Well you better start talking to me because I am your best bet for finding Mathew, who we both love immensely, James said.

"As I was saying, if birds and bees can use the process of magnetorecption, why can't we humans?" Maria asked.

"Is it because our own thoughts get in the way?" Jennifer replied.

"What are you teaching that girl, Maria? You want her to empty-headed so her mind is void of every thought that makes her an individual. Do you want the G.O.D. bots can get into her mind and program her, as one of them?" James asked.

"Of course not James. When we play our etherplayers, we are uniting electromagnetic fields with our own," Maria explained.

"You mean you are disrupting them," James said.

"Our intentions is to unify, to become one. When we play our music, we are able experience harmony which is in tune with the Life Forces surrounding us," Maria explained. "And it does one's heart good to hear the beautiful harmonic sound."

"Can I try, I could really use a lift at this moment," James said.

"Alright, you can try mine. Now, remember James, you are a living electrical charge interrupting the magnetic field of two antennas, so spread your feet apart slightly," Maria explained.

"Like this?" James asked.

"The vertical antenna is for pitch so move your hand back and forth and then just try moving your thumb and index finger. The horizontal antenna is for volume so you raise and lower your hand, then just do the same motion with your wrist, and see if you can play notes from this sheet," Maria explained.

"Actually that isn't bad," Jennifer said. "Now if you want to feel all the pain in the universe, keep your hand about eight inches from the horizontal loop antenna, which controls the volume and vibrate your hand around the vertical antenna which is controlling pitch. You can make it sound really spooky," Jennifer explained.

"That really sounds painful," James said.

"Maria, can you play 'Over the Rainbow', Maria makes the etherplayer sound like a woman is singing."

"That really sounds like a ghostly woman singing," James said.

"We know so little about the source of these forces, but they are always around us, vibrating, without us hearing them or seeing them, unless we can invent something to channel these forces to a frequency that is human friendly. We know the mechanics of these forces, but we really don't know the actual source, or if our input can actually inspire these forces to help us. We really don't know the power we would have, if all the forces around us, in conflict, actually united."

"Spinning magnets and electric currents are drivers of so many technologies we depend on. Without them we would feel useless because they empower us so much. We are stronger, and smarter and with these technologies we can do things a lot faster," Jennifer said.

"My hyper-loop rail service will be the fastest, the strongest, the smartest, and the first, if I don't let President Peel hold me back," James said.

"The force of nature shapes our lives and either strengthens or weakens our ability to channel energy," Maria said.

"The light, the magnetism and the power to keep all this life alive will be powerful enough to protect Mathew from evil, don't you think so, Mrs. Watson?" Jennifer asked.

"I do. We are more than just mere objects and the earth is much more than just a bunch of rocks, water, fire and air. Earth's beauty just takes your breath away, doesn't it? Many swear that when they connect to those higher forces with meditation and prayer they feel stronger and their problems seem much smaller," Maria explained.

"Maria do you really believe all that? In nature you have those horrible pecking orders that rule the food chain," James said.

"We all feed from the food chain," Jennifer said.

"Exactly my point, we are all at war with each other because we want to get the biggest piece of the pie before it is all eaten by someone else," James said.

"Come on James, it isn't all that bad. Not everything has to be a sum zero sport with a huge winner and a huge loser. Many people are just as happy to win a little so someone else can win something too," Maria said.

"You tell President Peel that. Of course it is all about sum zero games. I must be first, if my legacy changes the world overnight. The negative bias creates a shadow on the losing side, and slows it down, as a competitive disadvantage, and that is just the way it is. And President Peel isn't going to slow down my progress so that he can get ahead of me, and leave me behind in my own coal dust. To stay in the big leagues, and to be part and parcel of the 'Big Seven Coal Group's great super power, a player must win big, regardless of who loses big. The world is just one huge pecking order. It is not about who is right, it is all about who is in charge. That is the way of the world. For example look at all those bureaucratic cliques weaponizing systems and processes against other bureaucratic cliques on a global scale," James said. "They laugh at my Bering Strait Rail-Tube-Bridge Peace Complex while they put up walls, change traffic flows, and manage supply chains to benefit the few, while ordinary people are being forced by circumstance to live in degrading poverty. The only good thing about those walls that the G.O.D. bots are building will be how ingenious the human species will become as they try to find ways to tunnel under them. Maybe some of these people will be motivated to learn to work together again," James said.

"Look what happened to Mathew. He wasn't on guard. He was flyking around and did not consider his vulnerability. He didn't have a way of protecting his own personal space from the likes of Jethro and Bill. We are all at the mercy of the perpetual pecking order that is in continuous conflict with other pecking orders. And our love for Mathew, my immense love for my stepson, didn't matter to those controlling they system, at all," James said as he pushed aside a tear.

"I love Mathew immensely too, Mr. Coaltonstone," Jennifer said as she gave James a hug.

"You are just a child, Jennifer, what do you know about love?" James asked.

"I know how much it hurts to not know where Mathew is at this very moment. He has either been harmed or murdered by those two thugs you hired for security," Jennifer replied.

"I have tried to speak to someone in charge at the command station. There is no information at all concerning Mathew's search and rescue effort. All I am able to reach are those horrible depressing G.O.D. bots that put you on hold until a recording kicks in that says they are too busy to answer the phone," Maria said. "It has been over a day since Mathew was shot. We have to find him before it is too late."

"Yeah, I agree with you, Maria, or at least find what remains of him," James added.

"James, please. Listening to you talk about Mathew like that is upsetting," Maria said.

"They might as well be wearing one of those retro 'I don't care, do U?' jackets, because the collective of Government's Official Directors don't seem to care about anything except maintaining control over the masses and what they are thinking," Jennifer said.

"You are overdramatizing the situation, Jennifer, which is why you should never interrupt your elders," James scolded.

"Jennifer has a right to her opinion. Jennifer has as much at stake in this world as we do, and she will be staying in this world for a lot longer than us," Maria said.

"Speak for yourself, Maria, I am planning to live until I am at least a hundred and twenty-five," James said.

"Why?" Jennifer asked.

"Jennifer, you need to ask me why? I love being alive, and I have a lot of things I want to do. I want to experience the impact my Bering Strait Hyper-Loop rail Peace Complex has on the world once it takes off," James explained.

"I think it will be a real hit, especially for those old people who want to see the world really fast, before they die. Especially the old people who won't be living until they are past one hundred and twenty-five," Jennifer said.

"It would be nice though to be able to see out of the window and take in all the nature and scenery," Maria said

"There will be viewing screens, but the scenery will be whizzing by at around 600 MPH," James said.

"Only way you could possibly manage to live to be one hundred and twenty-five years old, would be if you became more robotic than human," Jennifer said. "I sure wouldn't want to live like that. It would be like selling your soul to the devil."

"I think James has done that already," Maria whispered to Jennifer. "Just look at what you young people will be inheriting, long after my generation has passed away," Maria said.

"Jennifer, Maria, I admit I have made some mistakes but I have accomplished a lot. I have never intentionally harmed anyone," James said.

"Well you dominate us all the time. Why can't you help us without dominating us in your typical patronizing style and condescending way? You make us so nervous and self-conscious when we try to talk to you seriously. It feels like you are purposely manufacturing social disabilities between us. You add insult to injury the same way those idiot G.O.D. bots do, the difference is, they are not human but you are. Those bots either leave you on hold, or repeat frivolous sentences mindlessly, telling you nothing and wasting your time as if our time were nothing," Maria said.

"I too can't stand the G.O.D. bots, but we can't dismiss why these G.O.D. bots are taking over. It is because the power cliques polarize everyone and everything until nothing is able to move or work without an autocrat in charge," James said.

"The autocratic G.O.D bots work as a team. They don't have egos to conflict with other egos. The G.O.D. bots are completely objective and are able to keep the system moving, without any human emotion. Our system and our economy are programmed to not freeze up in perpetual conflict and chaos, At least that is what we are taught in school," Jennifer said.

"We have heard the rhetoric many times. Maybe thousands of times. Thanks to our G.O.D. bots, our lives don't get frozen in time. Today, if we choose the winning side, we are able to move along and progress. The G.O.D. bots, in theory anyway, prevent human disasters because they are objective oriented and not ego oriented," James said.

"The sort of disaster that makes Pitville so famous," Jennifer asked.

"Talking about Pitville, when we find Mathew, should we bury him beside Ginger Goodwin or with his father, Mathew Watson Senior?"

"James, what a horrible question to be asking us right now. I suppose we will bury him next to his father," Maria responded angrily.

"The next question is where do we bury Christina, when the time comes? Next to Ginger or next to Mathew and Mathew's father? And what about baby James? He will always be fragile," James wondered out loud.

"James, my entire family, including Ginger, should be all together. Why isn't Ginger Goodwin buried in our family plot? Nobody asked us about our preferred arrangements before," Maria complained.

"Well I am asking you now. And another important question, is, do you know if Mathew had his identification card on him?" James said.

"Has, the word is has, Mr. Coaltonstone. I just know Mathew is still alive. I can feel his energy channeling around me," Jennifer said.

"That might be because he doesn't want to let go of all the things he is attached too," James said, trying to make a joke, but it just didn't come out right.

"James, please," Maria scolded.

"I am actually sort of repeating what Susan said, Jennifer's cousin, two times removed. All that I am saying is we need to be planning for the future. With or without closure," James said.

"We all know the first thing people like Bill and Jethro do to dehumanize someone is to destroy their identity, and for a child especially, could leave them very confused, demoralized and feeling empty and giving up. And once you give up, all hope is lost," Maria said.

"Tell me about it, I mean those cliques at school are bad enough and those horrible mean kids who deliberately make you lose your place while you are trying to read by playing word games or making all kinds of noises," Jennifer said.

"And then I bet the teacher will then assume that you are dim witted, angry or suffer from some hyper active disorder because you spoke out of turn and acted yourself," James said.

"I suppose you are right James, but that is not the fault of nature, it is the fault of the choices that are made by the ones with the most social power in our society and sub-societies," Maria said.

"I will let you in on a secret. I have rights to my coal mines that are under occupied properties and I have been granted permission to convert the mines that are closed weather resistant condos," James said.

"Are you kidding?" Jennifer and Maria asked at the same time.

"Absolutely not," James said. "Do you think it is even practical to be living above the ground in this day and age, with all these strange weather events going on at a moment's notice? You just can't blame nature anymore."

"So you actually agree that it could be Mina or possibly our side is weaponizing cloud seeding or what have you, Mr. Coaltonstone?" Jennifer asked.

"I don't agree or disagree," James said.

"What nature creates between the cycles of growth and decay strive for some kind of balance. And all these conflicts are bound to imbalance the natural order of things, These crazy power cliques and their internal power struggles are hurting each other and everyone stuck in the middle," Maria said as she wished that she could do more to defend Mother Earth. "In nature the cycles continue through us, around us and despite of us," Maria added.

"If it were up to these crazy power cliques, they would shut down all the engines of the world and claim that the risk of free trade is too high of a security risk," James said.

"As the global economies crash in unison, and millions of people die in all these senseless conflicts, wars and famines, the power cliques then, after playing God with other people's lives, often just close their eyes in prayer, and claim innocence," Maria said.

"If I didn't know it to be true I would have thought it all was a bad dystopian fiction story line," James said.

"Mothers always get blamed for their children's misdeeds. Blaming power politics on Mother Earth is not fair," Jennifer said.

"Well what about Cold Feet Mountain breaking apart and crumbling on part of Coalton Two and burying over seventy people? Whose fault was that?" Jennifer asked.

"Don't forget the bank. The mountain managed to bury Coalton Two's First Bank," James said,

"You only have yourself and the Big Seven Coal Group's reckless mining culture for that one," Maria said.

"It is just fake news poisoning your mind, Maria. The Big Seven Coal Group gets picked on all the time whenever there is a natural disaster beyond our control. We get picked on because we are the super power of mining," James replied.

CHAPTER 9:

Can Young Blood Slow down Aging?

March 18th 2031, around 1:00 PM: "You don't understand,"

James yelled over his telecom to John Bell, "I don't care about branding. I need rejuvenation, right now."

"Sir, I understand. We are sending you some product as we speak. Nevertheless, we need to brand your product, to optimize your profits, to build trust. This is a great product and we are growing distribution channels like you wouldn't believe," John replied.

"Okay, Okay, we will call it JC. I know it is a great product. I need the rejuvenation right now," James said.

"Sir, should we brand it 'Rejuvenation JC'?" John asked.

"Sounds like a great idea. Make the JC stand out so people can call it something quick, like they do with TP," James said.

"Understood," John replied.

"The product makes you feel like you can live for ever, the way I used to feel when I was young."

"Then should I use that as the slogan, Sir, 'JC makes you feel like you can live forever'?

"Yes, that would be a very catchy slogan, John," James said.

Is that all then, Sir?" John asked.

"No, there is one more thing. I need a personal supply of JC sent to my Coalton Two office, immediately," James said.

"We have already sent your supply to your Pitville address," John said.

"John, you made a mistake then. I feel old, and I need a supply of JC sent to my Coalton Two office, right away. I need the supply to be flown in, now. I must stay sharp. John, can you hear me? I need to hear your reply," James said.

"Sir, our visibility is terrible, and the winds are torrential. We would be safer for our workers and our product if we used the train and tunnels, Sir," John said.

"John, can you just do what I say. And tell the foreman down there to keep those kids from crying and banging on their cages. Increase their dose if you have to," James commanded.

"Sir, it is not advisable to increase their dose. It will make the product less potent," John said.

"Okay, then gag them with duck tape and chain them. We have to stop those kids from crying and banging their heads on their cages," James ordered.

"I understand, Sir," John said. "Sir, did you hear about the prison riots? Prisoners are organizing across Tut territory. They refuse to work, some refuse to eat and others are tearing the prisons apart, burning whatever they can," John said.

"That is President Peel's problem, not mine. I have a serious problem that we can't kill. I saw Dianne, the PPZ newscaster, publicly broadcasting the entrance to the ancient cave that was mostly unknown until today. You know, that flooded out area behind the back wall of this facility," James said.

"Do you want me to duck tape and chain her too, then? Would serve her right for all the fake news she generates. Isn't that right, Sir?" John asked.

"We'll see," James replied. "Did your soldiers get their fingertip work done, as discussed earlier?" James asked.

"Yes Sir, there will be no fingerprints, Sir," John promised.

"What about Mayor Stern?" John asked.

"We'll see about that too," James replied. "We want to stay friendly."

"As in friendly fire, Sir?" John asked.

"I was thinking we should do what we always do. Have our little meetings, discuss things and then go ahead with what we always do as if Mayor Stern's power only exists on paper," James said.

"You mean we create a paper trail going one way and then do what we do without any paper trail?" John asked.

"Exactly," James replied.

CHAPTER 10:

Who Is STONEWALLING?

March 18th 2031, around 2:30 PM:

"It is like this black cloud grows directly over my head. The thunder and lightning remind me there is a greater power up there," Maria said.

"This global warming and the increase in violence is the perfect atmosphere for war. One day it is super muggy and the next day it is so cold people are freezing to death as they wait for a bus to go to their low paying jobs. The extremes make people more animal like, don't you think, Mr. Coaltonstone?" Jennifer asked.

"I suppose they do. There is nothing worse than feeling muggy and heavy with sweat unless you feel like you are about to freeze to death. All kinds of things exploit the beast in man and a lot of things elevate man too," James replied.

"It really scares me when men like Jethro and Bill are given the power to play God. That scares me almost as much as this global fad to seed clouds, regardless of how many toxins the clouds may be carrying," Maria said.

"I guess you heard that a group of transient orcas tipped Jethro and Bill's submarine over, when it surfaced. The crewmembers were going to do some fishing and landed up surrounded by orcas. The orcas acted very angry and according to authorities, odd, when they tipped over their submarine while the hatch was open and the water damage was significant," James said.

"Wow. I never heard anything about that. Why do they call the orcas transient?" Jennifer asked.

"I don't know. The whales appear to be settling down and were actually acting like owned the place," Maria said.

"I thought they were free to swim around where ever they please and settle down wherever they please. Was anyone hurt? I haven't being watching the news. I have been getting lost in my thoughts," Jennifer said.

"No, amazingly no one was hurt. There are a lot of protesters and counter-protesters though. They may hurt each other. One side is waving signs that say 'SAVE THE WHALES' and the other side is waving signs that say 'SAVE THE HUMANS'. There was a lot of damage to the submarine and it was taken into dry dock at Tut Naval Shipyard. Jethro and Bill and the whole crew had to be rescued, but they are fine and will be issued a newer sub with even more fire power," James said.

"How scary is that?" Jennifer said.

"Very scary," James replied.

"Someone took a video, and they put it on 'You Tube'. Look, I have it right here. I have never seen anything like it before. And look at the headline, 'LOCAL MILITARY SUBMARINE ATTACKED BY A MOB OF ANGRY TRANSIENT WHALES'," Maria said.

"My God the orcas look a lot smarter than Jethro and Bill, don't they?" Jennifer said.

"Of course they do and a lot more powerful. Orcas are incredibly intelligent creatures. The paralimbic cleft and super-developed lobes are beyond our scientific scope, possibly because our human brain is far less developed. The orca has so many more folds in their brains than we do. We underestimate how smart they really are, it is amazing how smart they are. Their gyrification index is 5.7 compared to the 2.2 for us mere human mortals," Maria said.

"And who knows if Jethro and Bill's brains are even as highly developed as the average brain," Jennifer said.

"Jennifer, really. You know it is the culture that keeps those boys narrow minded, not their ability, and who knows how the lack of making connections, over time, stunts brain development," Maria said.

"I guess you are right, Mrs. Watson, but avoiding the task of making connections over the years probably does change the wiring of a person's brain, just like the way you say," Jennifer said.

"And the opposite is being applied to the whales. My guess is that due to the great and beautiful Orca culture, those creatures are probably ten times more capacity to act intelligently than any one of us, especially Jethro and Bill," Maria said.

"And we have the gull to call such creatures transient and label them with identifying Ids that sound like a chemical we include in process food, adding insult to injury. We act as if we have the right to shove these creatures into fish tanks for our own personal entertainment and convenience. We treat these ancient inhabitants of the seas as if they are encroaching on us when we are really encroaching on them. The oceans are the orcas' home. The orca's sixth sense, and ability to communicate with each other, is beyond our comprehension, let alone Jethro's and Bill's," Maria said.

"I am sure whales hate all those wartime navy sonar drills, you really can't blame them," Jennifer said.

"There have been reports that whales often get stranded while trying to escape the sonar noise. There have been other reports that whales change their depth so rapidly when escaping the sonar noise, they start bleeding from their eyes and ears," Maria said.

"Those whales are so amazing. I can see why Mathew loved photographing them and being as close to them as he could. He really loved those whales. He sometimes said that he thought the whales were trying to communicate to him, He used to say they were thanking him for not being a predator," Jennifer said.

"I hate to change the subject but I see more black clouds coming. This bad weather is never ending. Whenever those black clouds grow directly over my head I sometimes think of the great power of nature and how dynamic it is. And sometimes I wonder if they are fake clouds, just a product of cloud seeding. I feel so alienated from the world I live, I can't imagine what it would be like to have a sixth sense similar to that of a whale or a bird?" Maria said.

"Having such a supernatural power would drive a person crazy. Whenever I see black clouds, I think of lightning, thunderstorms and hail and the cost of my house and business insurance going up," James said.

"James, can't you see how wonderful and magical nature is?" Maria asked.

"Not really. I have been teaming up with a cloud seeding initiative, which will be sending chemical flares into clouds to suppress ice crystallisation which forms hail," James said.

"I thought you were against cloud seeding, Mr. Coaltonstone," Jennifer said.

"I have been convinced that this particular cloud seeding initiative could be quite profitable and benefit mankind, I mean peoplekind, dear. We make it rain, instead of hail and the local authorities filter the water when it arrives through our pipe. And then this water will be diluted with the available water supply, whatever that might be. Often in the regions we are considering to sell our water to have serious water shortages. It is not like here, where we have so much water. Tut Metropolis is able to install water fountains into some of the main sidewalks, to cool the citizenry during these reoccurring extreme heat waves. Not all places are as lucky as we are," James said.

"Sounds very risky," Maria said.

"We are planning to do good work, Maria," James said.

"When have I heard that before?" Maria replied.

"People drink our water they trust it and it is needed, and the demand is only going to grow greater. The water shortage is getting worse every day, and no one owns clouds. If I don't harvest them, someone else will," James said.

"James has anyone ever told you how accident prone you are?" Maria asked.

"Not to his face, I bet," Jennifer interjected.

"Jennifer, really," Maria scolded.

"We have the technology to seed clouds but not to control how much rain comes out of them, I acknowledge that. But practice will make perfect. One day we will a great and beautiful rain making system, which will make Tut great again and will be the envy of the world. We will pipe this water to places that need it the most. This is one of my dreams that I hope I will actualize in my lifetime," James said.

"You mean you are going to seed clouds, brand them with your signature and then pipe the water to regions that will pay the most?" Jennifer asked.

"Exactly Jennifer. I will be reducing water stress due to climate change and bring goodwill and peace to the global village," James said

"You are kidding?" Maria asked.

"I certainly am not. I am going to make a difference. I could live for another 40 years or more. I can brand this product the way I brand all my products. My ideas work, and that is why I make everything great again," James said. "All we do is fly above the cloud line, and drop a payload of dry ice and salt and silver iodide or we flares chemicals into the clouds. It depends. We are trying different methods until we find the best one to use. As it rains, we send the water through our beautiful and great pipe to regions that need the water, and are willing to pay a premium price for it," James explained.

"How do you get the water before it floods the population and all their stuff living below the clouds you seed?" Jennifer asked.

"Sometimes we get a cloud that rains and gives us the optimum amount of water that we need, and the process is very manageable. Sadly, there are times the cloud rains too much water and the water does cause flood damage below. Mother Nature has the same problem, so no one is perfect. We try our best. When our best is not good enough, we don't admit that we just seeded that cloud. Who would ever admit to that? When our experiment goes badly, we just blame the entire fiasco on Mother Nature. Who doesn't blame bad weather on Mother Nature?" James asked.

CHAPTER 11:

Tunnels, Bridges and Awakenings

March 18th 2031, around 3:00 PM: "Bobby, do you have the cargo all prepared?" James asked Bobby.

"Yes, Sir, I do," Bobby Coaltonstone replied.

"And you are aware that these transactions are all about our national security, and more importantly, about our family security? Our family comes first, always,"

"Yes Sir, I understand. Our family comes first, exactly the way it should be," Bobby replied.

"This is why I have you and Alex in charge of these two newest projects, my hyper-loop train and tunnel network, and the ten cars of cargo. We own the first hyper-loop freight train system and we will be the first to cross the Bering Strait and the first to link North America with Eurasia. I wish we could have performed this historical journey more publicly, but this is all mine, no one, not even President Peel will take any of this away from me. You and your brother will be the first to make this journey, and this journey will be the greatest ride of your life and of this century. You are Coaltonstones and it is your birthright to be first and to be great. And one day we will be free again to share this technology with the world. Time is money, so the time we will be saving in shipping costs will easily make up for the cost of this greatest and most beautiful hyper-loop rail network ever built and that we will ever see in our lifetime. I am not going to let a stupid war and a stupid president ruin my dream. Peel thinks he is so great while he humiliates everyone beneath him, but he will never humiliate me by trying to nationalize my property and especially not my hyper-loop rail network. I would rather give it all to Mina than give it to him," James said.

"Yes Sir, I understand," Bobby said.

"My hyper-loop rail service will be a great ride, son," James said.

"Sir, you know I am claustrophobic, do you think I am the right person to be riding into the future like this, in a capsule, at 600 MPH," Bobby asked.

"Just be tough and act like the boss. Your actions might even save the republic, one day," James said.

"Do you think they will name a town after me, if I give them a beautiful water fountain like Alex did?" Bobby asked.

"They just might, son, they just might. Alex will be with you as you ride into the future. There will be viewing screens and you will be amazed how beautiful that part of the world is," James said.

"Sir, you don't think watching the scenery speed past at 600 MPH make me sick in the stomach?" Bobby asked.

"Make sure you have a bag with you and keep your work area neat and tidy. The ride will be so fast, you won't ever think of looking back. You will be protected and safe as you speed through the hyper-loop tunnel, leaving all that unpleasantness, in Tut territory behind you. You always said that you wanted a revolution well this it. And every revolutionary must be brave and love freedom. As you ride into the future you will be leaving all those naysayers behind, rotting while they keep themselves suspended in their self-made chaotic hell. You must not be heard by anyone who might recognize your voice, even though your disguise is very good, we couldn't find a way to disguise your voice so it stayed natural sounding. Alex has a very good disguise too. You will see. I am emailing you a picture of Alex in his disguise, as we speak," James said as he fumbled with the send button. Bobby received Alex's picture almost at the speed of light.

"Yes, Sir, I just received the picture, he looks much older. I would have never recognized him, Sir," Bobby said.

"You both look a lot older. I wouldn't have recognized you, either," James said as he took another look at Bobby's picture and then stared at his screen. "Your voice sounds the same though. I would recognize your voice anywhere and others might recognize your voice too, and put two and two together, if they were thinking and realized that you have gone AWOL Most people don't think anymore. Only a few people are making any connections while thinking, but it will take only one person to uncover your identity, then your mission will be over, so don't underestimate anyone, and especially not fools. Bobby, stay vigilant especially around John Bell, he takes the Brotherhood's side in most arguments. Ono will be meeting you on the other side. He will be one of the few associates who will know who you are and he loves my hyper-loop rail project, just as much as we do," James said.

"Good, I trust Ono with my life," Bobby said.

"Well you better, because that is exactly what you will be doing," James replied.

"And you are sure all ten cars will fit in the hyper-loop rail network, while our bots repair the mountain, from within?" Bobby asked. Seeing the look on James face through his com-screen, Bobby quickly added that he would make sure that all ten cars would fit.

"Very good, you are the engineer in the family," James said. "I am depending on your engineering skills, son, so don't forget who you are and how important this project is to human development. I plan to move forward even if President Peel finds it easier to move backward."

"Sir, what happens if someone stops us at the border or walks in on us?"

"You will be travelling so fast and so deep under the ground, there will be no access to borders, all they will feel is shaking. We are moving black clouds over head, and will pour rain on strategic locations. Those idiots who said 'anybody but Coaltonstone', and especially those who wore those buttons, when they went out to vote, will have no idea what is going on. You and the cargo will be protected. And those people will be running for shelter. We are the future and are leaving those losers behind us. And remember, son, don't play that new shoot-em-up up' game," James warned.

"Why, Dad?" Bobby asked.

"Don't 'why Dad me?' just don't play it. And don't worry about those losers up above. How are people who live like dogs in shacks going to agree on anything enough to do anything meaningful? Anyway, John is still taking care of all of the minor security issues on this side of the wall, so be careful around him, and avoid contact with him. Remember, if John tries to act like your boss, isn't. I am the one who is in charge of this operation. John wouldn't even be able to understand the importance of uniting Eurasian with North America, and soften our culture but not our minds. Those Pitville miners are harmless and they fall all over each other during their petty arguments, especially when their fragile egos get bruised. Those people will never be a match against the Brotherhood, let alone our global oligopoly, which now includes the greatest rail system ever built. Linking Eurasia with North America, is one of the last greatest feats left, and I will be the one to do it. I will net let that megalomaniac Peel pull me backwards. We are moving towards the brightest future that we can make for ourselves," James said.

"You mean the bright light at the end of the tunnel?" Bobby asked.

"Exactly, we are the ones who drive the future, not petty, narrow minded politicians and their two dimensional, centralized agendas. We are the producers, we create the dream and the steam that fires up most of the engines that run this world. Those people in the Exclusion League, feed off us," James said.

"I suppose you are right, Sir. The people who are colluding with us enjoy higher prices, so why would they betray us? Everyone else is pretty much powerless and helpless and they know how futile it is to resist. Maybe they will protest against each other. No one avoids and hates the doomed more than the already doomed. You always tell me that, and I observe it every day, for myself," Bobby said.

"You can say that again, Bobby. You are right and so am I. Never forget how right we are to be moving forward with our assets, and leave those losers behind. I say good riddance," James said.

"I will say that again, good riddance. They put me through hell, and now I am back stronger than I ever was before," Bobby replied.

"That is exactly how our power works. The poor stay poor, and when they are no longer sustainable they die off, while the rich just get richer. And one day, our power will grow to become interplanetary and then we, the Coaltonstones will be fueling the space of force of nations," James said.

"What about our workers?" Bobby asked.

"What about them? If we need them, we can email them. Those people's destinies have been set at birth because we pave their paths from the moment of birth. We put the boys in boy clothes and girls in girl clothes. They cling to the rope we give them to cling on to, when they go out on group walks while still toddlers, and they continue to cling onto that rope for the rest of their lives. Once in a while, the odd one will hang themselves with that little piece of rope we gave them. We define those people and classify those people and when we need to drive them crazy we flip the glass ceiling over and we trap them in a world of smoke and mirrors and then condemn them because thrash about violently, like a trapped rat. The mirrors reflect all the failures and disappointments their programmed destinies dished out to them. Their fates were already sealed. Their fake identities were stamped into their psyche and their despair grows to be overwhelming, they will take the easy way out, and die with less dignity than dogs. They vote for oligarchs all the time because what other choice do they have?" James asked.

"No other choice, Sir," Bobby replied.

"And now the oligarch they voted for claims to be their judge, juror and executioner, but he won't be mine," James said.

"Exactly! How many of those people have been excluded from social mobility since birth? And how many federal workers will not be getting their promised pay raise which was supposed to be equal to the rise in the cost of living index?" James asked.

"Most of them," Bobby replied.

"President Peel says he fears violence from the opposition and he is threatening to starve his own workers whose paychecks are being eaten up by hyperinflation," James said.

"Those are the people that voted for Peel," Bobby said.

"Exactly, he betrays even those people who voted for him. The Minese, especially the undocumented ones, are raised in collectives, sometimes relocated and retrained in collectives, and then at the end of their short life they are discarded as collectives. Once we force the Minese into retirement, it is too late for them to build a new life for themselves, as an individual. The Minese, the documented and the illegals are left to claw at each other in a futile effort to escape their destinies. Forever trapped in the dark caves of this planet. What hope do they have? " James said.

"No hope, Sir. The lucky ones who have a place above ground may hope to see the moon and stars at night," Bobby replied.

"And we were destined to be included in the Firestone Organization at birth. We are all products of some form of social engineering, or another. Ours is just superior," James said.

"And luckier," Bobby said.

"Life is all about the cards you are dealt. You take the card and run with it, just like we are planning to do with our precious cargo," James said.

Have you ever tried the initiation rites that the New Bloods are required to perform before they are allowed to join?" Bobby asked.

"No, we will never have to perform such stunts, because we are members of the Old Bloods. I don't even know if I could walk on hot coals but I do know I would never want to," James confessed.

"Me neither. I love watching the ceremony, though. It is amazing how the New Bloods psyche themselves out and actually complete the Firestone Walk," Bobby said.

"I have never been one for secret handshakes, secret words and secret rites in general," James said.

"But you have belonged to the Firestones since birth, just like Alex and I have," Bobby said.

"Yes, because I thrive on the culture. Would you rather hang out with people who are struggling all the time, just to make ends meet? James asked.

"Of course not!" Bobby replied.

"They look like dregs, they feel like dregs, and that is who and what they are. Remember Bobby, you are not a dreg. You are not being purged. Never forget who you are. You are a Coaltonstone and an Old Blood Firestone. You are my son and the G.O.D. Bots are programmed to leave you alone," James replied.

"You mean, I am your second son," Bobby said.

"I have never made that distinction," James retorted.

"I have a question. Why don't more illegals and vagrants just kill themselves, the way the Buynese do, when they are overwhelmed by helplessness and feelings of despair?" Bobby asked.

"Because we, people like you and me, give them hope. They are dependent on us, and we are dependent on them, though not as much. The Buynese are conditioned to feel as if they are born alone to die alone. They are attractive to other Buynese only when they have good jobs, wear designer clothes and drive the latest model of vehicle. When all those things are gone, so are their friends and family. The illegals and vagrants have nothing to lose and seem to be happy enough going from one promised opportunity to another promised opportunity. They don't seem to care when all their opportunities fan out, but I do. Their hope for a better future is what drove them to Tut Island in the first place and their hope for a better future is what keeps them here. So why are we missing the opportunity to prevent war? Why are we missing the opportunity to see the positive force in all these people? For the Minese immigrant, legal and illegal, hope is totally faith based. And the miners, who are able to vote, didn't really vote for President Peel and his Exclusion League backers, they voted for the more doomed to be condemned. The legal immigrants voted against the illegals, because what choice did they have? The illegals and the vagrants are the ones they have to compete against," James said, again.

"So you are saying that the legal immigrants voted for President Peel and his Exclusion League backers because they don't want to compete with the illegal immigrants or the vagrants for the few mining jobs that are open to them?" Bobby asked.

"Partly, they also voted for a dictator so they could feel certainty and my guess is that they also like their hatred being validated. The state of the unknown can rattle the nerves at times, but hatred without validation, can make a person feel terribly guilty and bitter. When people were expecting something better out of life than they actually got, scapegoats made them feel less of a failure. The Exclusion League validates those feelings. A dictator tells people what is and what is going to be, but he will also give people permission to hate, openly," James said.

"So they voted for President Peel hoping that the exclusion of the illegal immigrants and vagrants would benefit them personally?" Bobby asked.

"I am actually surprised that President Peel won the election. I thought that I was going to win," James said.

"I think everyone was surprised. Some think the election was rigged. I think that sometimes, too. People know they can't fight and win any conflict they might face once the G.O.D. bots are in charge. It's self-defeating to vote for a dictator though. I voted for you, Dad," Bobby said.

"Thank you son. I voted for myself too. President Peel is more than just a dictator, he is a validator. There is no one more unforgiving to the doomed than the slightly less doomed. President Peel's tweets are crazy but they are able to validate craziness, because Peel is the president of the entire Tut territory and his opinions are taken seriously. And if my campaign had carried a harder line, I would have won. I promised jobs, which wasn't enough. President Peel validated negative feelings in the hardened masses and gave them permission to hate openly which in turn lowers their own expectations for higher quality of life," James said.

"Where do you think our former workers will stay? Where will they live?" Bobby asked.

"I have no idea. We moved all the Pitvilian shacks that we own, to Coalton Two. We needed quick replacements when Cold Feet Mountain buried some of the homes. So technically our former employees are now homeless. If they are not careful they could be condemned to walk upon this earth as dregs for the rest of their lives. The militia will label them transients and they will be channeled by the G.O.D. bots and purged out of town and maybe even out of existence. Soon they will look and be treated no differently than the illegals and vagrants are," James said.

"Why can't we just build enough shacks, so every family who needs one, can have one?" Bobby asked.

"Because those people didn't vote for me. They voted for Peel. We don't owe those people anything. They are no longer our responsibility or worry. Let the government take care of them. Scarcity keeps people needing and wanting. President Peel and his Exclusion League backers are in charge now, not me," James said.

"Could the Pitvilian miners move into the tunnels under Pitville, the way the Minese miners do? That would be ironic wouldn't it?" Bobby asked.

"I doubt it. The Pitvilian miners are a different breed, they like to see the light at the end of the day, even if it is just moonlight. Anyway some of those tunnels are going to be renovated into fancy condos and the illegals will have to find somewhere else to hide like rodents," James said.

"Those people will have nothing left to stay for in Pitville, but they stay anyway, why?"

"Because they feel at home in Pitville, even though they will be homeless and outsiders will see them as nothing more than vagrants, regardless if they are immigrants or migrants. We own everything and they know no other life. We are the ones who come first, in Pitville and everywhere else that our Oligarch maintains power. And these days, our business model is the only model that works because it is sustainable. Our way of life makes a lot of sense. Buy low and sell high," James said.

"I still can't imagine what the Pitvillians, who aren't Minese, are going to do now that they are homeless. We have moved their shacks to Coalton Two..." Bobby was saying before he is father cut him off.

"Our shacks. We moved our shacks to Coalton Two. If they wanted us to help them, they would have voted for me," James interrupted.

"Yes, we moved our shacks, so now they probably will hate the Minese even more than they used to because they will see them as fierce competitors, not just for their jobs but for their homes too. More importantly, they might start hating us," Bobby said.

"They probably already hate us, or they would have voted for me. That is why we need the Brotherhood watching those people, and when necessary we infiltrate their ranks. The rule of autocratic oligarchs is the rule of law. We own the economic system so we own the necessities of life wherever we hold power on Earth. We all understand that. How do you think Peel won? President Peel is just as much an oligarch as we are. Peel owns a good chunk of our shares, and his shares are protected in one of those blind trust funds. Those blind trust funds are meant to fool the financially illiterate, but they can't fool other oligarchs. Mob rule functions by default especially when no one can agree on anything. The doomed will just claw away at the more doomed, and nothing much will get done. One side will target the other side, voicing opposite opinions, and both sides are conditioned to have extremely fragile egos that are easily bruised, so they are programmed to act like ticking time bombs. The political climate is so polarized that only an autocratic, egoless G.O.D. bot will be able to get anything done. There is a huge opportunity cost when nothing gets done, and everyone knows it," James said.

"Hold on Bobby I have another call coming in. It is Doctor Knight. I will make it quick," James promised.

"I am still wondering where the Pitville miners are going to live and whether they are going to hate us more than they hate the Minese miners," Bobby said but James had already put him on hold.

"Hello," James said as he answered his other line.

"Mr. Coaltonstone, it is Doctor Knight. I have very good news. Christina just woke up. She needs rest, but her pulse is much stronger, her vital signs are good, though she is still very weak," Doctor Ashley Knight explained.

"That is wonderful news, what should I do now? How is little James?" James asked.

"I can't stress enough that both Christina and baby James need normalcy, stability, and fewer shocks to their systems," Ashley said.

"Of course, I certainly understand. I will be right there," James said.

"I am not sure if that is a good idea, at the moment, Mr. Coaltonstone," Ashley said.

"I must go back, I belong there. Christina is my wife. James is my son. I belong there," James protested.

"Sometimes you need to let others feel like they belong too, Mr. Coaltonstone," Ashley explained.

"I understand that. I love Christina and little James," James said.

"Christina and baby James need rest and cannot be exposed to any new stressors, or they both could suffer a relapse," Ashley replied.

"I see," James said.

"You must let nature take its course," Ashley said.

"I understand," James said.

"Do you?" Ashley said.

"Of course I do. I thought Christina was never going to wake up. I am so thankful that Christina is still alive. You are such a good Doctor, Ashley. Probably one of the best in Tut," James said.

"Can I be blunt, Mr. Coaltonstone?" Ashley asked.

"Absolutely, Ashley," James replied.

"You can't go back to the ship and start driving Christina crazy again," Ashley said.

"Again? I would never do that?" James said in protest.

"Maybe not on purpose, but you drive me crazy, at times. Like I said before, both Christina and baby James cannot undergo any new stressors, not for a while," Ashley said.

"Another thing, Mr. Coaltonstone, Christina is calling out for Mathew. What do I tell her?" Ashley asked.

"I don't know," James said before he broke down and cried.

THE END

Stay Tuned for Book Six!

Produced by S.E. McKenzie Productions
First Print Edition September 2016

Enquiries: 1(778)992-2453
Mailing Address:
S. E. McKenzie Productions
168 B 5th St.
Courtenay, BC
V9N 1J4

Email Address:
messidartha@aol.com

http://www.amazon.com/SarahMcKenzie/e/B00H9RWX48/

www.ingramcontent.com/pod-product-compliance
Lightning Source LLC
Chambersburg PA
CBHW060155130626
46556CB00006B/2655